INTO THE
OCEAN

INTO THE
OCEAN

Stanton McCaffery

NEW PULP PRESS

Published by New Pulp Press, LLC, 926 Truman Avenue, Key West, Florida 33040, USA.

For information contact:
Publisher@NewPulpPress.com

ISBN-13: 978-1945734106 (New Pulp Press)

ISBN-10: 1945734108

Printed in the United States of America
Visit us on the web at www.newpulppress.com

INTO THE
OCEAN

CHAPTER 1

Brett stomps holes in the mud. He kicks downed branches out of his way. His hammer is in his hand, held to his side. Flies and mosquitos are buzzing around him, getting in his eyes and his ears, fueling his rage even more. His skin is sticky with sweat and grime left over from his workday.

The Jersey swamp weather is one more thing that reminds him of his childhood, how his father would complain about it and say it made him feel like he was in the tropics instead of the northeast. There's the Turnpike too, and the constant buzz of traffic and horns, the industrial smells. There's the fence topped with razor wire at the edge of the wooded park. And ten feet in front of him, tripping on roots and occasionally running full speed into trees, there's the bloodied teenage boy trying to escape.

Carved into the wooden handle of Brett's hammer, towards the top, are the initials "J.B." Towards the bottom, on the same side, are the initials "B.B." The hammer's held so tightly in his hands that his fingers are pink. He uses the tool during the day for work, fixing things. He uses it at night to fix people.

The kid falls again and looks behind him at Brett who's approaching patiently like he's a masked villain from a slasher movie. Brett finds satisfaction in his terror. The look on the kid's face tells him that it's working. It usually does.

Edging closer now, Brett's only a few steps away. The kid has flopped on his back and is trying to get as far away as possible. He's kicking his feet and mud is flying everywhere, some of it into his own mouth. His Rutgers football T-shirt has mud on it. Brett can see the team logo illuminated in the dark by lights from the Turnpike and remembers hearing how the kid is some star athlete, that he has already been picked up for college ball. Now is the perfect time to teach him how to act, before he gets too out of control, too big to handle even for Brett.

There's a trickle of blood running down from the kid's mouth to his chin. He must have cut himself on a tree branch or hit his face on something when he fell. There's a thick red cut in the middle of his lip that makes Brett think of the scar on his own face. It's a pink strip of bumpy flesh that starts at his right cheekbone and works its way straight down to the top of his jaw line. During the day, and in most of his interactions with people, Brett's so conscious of the scar. He worries that people are staring at it, mocking him to themselves. But during these activities, whether he's alone or with Nate, he doesn't try to hide it. He uses the tool on his face given to him by the past to build their fear. They should be afraid of him, he wants the scar to say. They should be afraid of the consequences of their actions.

"Who are you?" the kid says. His adult body would have anyone believe he's on the manhood side of puberty, but the cracking of his voice says there's still growing left to do. There's a tree behind him that he backs into. Nowhere to run to, baby. Nowhere to hide.

Brett takes slow motion steps forward, attempting to make the kid so afraid he's on the brink of passing out. But Brett's not going to let him. A message needs to get across.

"I'm what happens when you fuck with people," says Brett. He deliberately deepens his voice, makes it gravely. "Now I want you to tell me where the pictures are at."

Squinting his eyes, the kid says, in his shaking leaf voice, "W...what pictures?" He shakes his head so hard it looks ready to spin around on his neck. "I don't know what you're talking about, man."

A crow squawks loudly on a tree branch and the kid looks up, startled. Brett keeps his eyes in front of him. On the Turnpike, nearby, a tractor-trailer rides over the rumble strip. The kid tries to kick him in the crotch but Brett catches his foot, twists it a little and shoves it aside.

"You're not gonna want to do that, alright. And don't play fucking dumb with me either. You know damn well what I'm talking about. The ones of the girl."

No response. Just shaking. Brett lifts the hammer from his side. "Don't be shy."

"They're on my ph... phone." He reaches into the pocket of his dirtied basketball shorts and pulls out a large white phone with a crack down the middle of the screen.

Brett looks at it. The thing must cost more than his truck. He extends his hand. The kid quickly gives it to him and pulls away.

"Where else you got 'em?"

"That's it. That's it. I wasn't going to do anything with them."

Brett smirks. He knows it makes his scar more prominent. "I'm not the person you want to lie to." The half-smile vanishes from his face and he moves closer. "Understand?"

The kid nods his head up and down. A sudden smell of piss is in the air.

The picture on the front screen of the phone is of him in his football uniform, posing by a goal post with a ball in his arms and a look of determination and confidence in his eyes. Brett thinks back to what his own life was like when he was that age and then he drops the phone into the mud. He raises his hammer, has his fingers wrapped around the carved initials towards the bottom, and brings it down on the phone. He does it again and again.

"I better not hear about you again. I better not hear about you talkin' to that girl. And I sure as hell better not hear about those pictures ever the fuck again. If I do, I promise you you'll regret it for the rest of your fucking life.

Got it?"

The kid is crying. "Yeah. Yeah."

Brett takes his hammer and taps the kid's knee. "Nobody's gonna want a receiver with a shattered knee, alright." He pauses, then stares into his eyes without blinking. "Now get the fuck out of here."

Leaving his home state of New Jersey is always pleasant. The open air of northeastern Pennsylvania, which he's now driving into, a little west and north of the Poconos and all the tourists and rich folk, is so much better. It allows Brett to breathe, to be calm, to get away from the past. As much as he dislikes the Garden State, he goes back when he has to.

When he reaches his cabin he gets out of his truck and stretches him arms, takes in a deep breath. He walks up the steep gravel driveway.

The cabin is surrounded by oaks and sycamores and weeds that have grown into trees. Some are dead and about to fall over. There's an owl that lives in one of them and at night it hoots.

When he climbs the steps and goes inside Al greets him. The cat rubs against his leg and meows a loud hungry cry. Brett rubs his head with both hands. "I know, pal. I know."

He's a grey cat with a white diamond on his chest and white paws. He has only a quarter of a tail and a lame eye. Brett found him as a kitten at a job site, tearing through a garbage bag, shivering, shit caked on his back legs.

Brett walks to the fridge and Al follows, howling all the way. The only thing inside the fridge is cat food and protein shakes. He feeds Al and then himself.

The cabin is one open space and a bathroom. No bed, just a futon. There's no heat or AC, only a wood-burning stove. There are bookshelves everywhere, and more books than can even fit on them all. Some are stacked on the floor. On top of one shelf is a picture in a cheap plastic frame.

Brett is twenty years younger in it. He's wearing a green polo shirt and has on a big grin. There's no scar. He's surrounded by four other people. Two of them are dead now.

His cell phone is underneath the futon where he put it before he went out. There are three missed calls and three messages. It's routine. Always the same calls and the same messages. One call and corresponding message is from his boss, Fred, telling him where the job site is for tomorrow. One is from Nate, his friend and partner in crime. He'll get back to Nate, just not tonight. The other call he won't return.

CHAPTER 2

"**H**ow about instead of the one dish for five dollars, you give me the two of them for seven," says the old lady at the thrift store across the counter from Sarah. The woman brings a hand to her mouth and coughs. It sounds as if she smokes two packs every half hour. Sarah rolls her eyes even though she knows she shouldn't. Her father always told her not to let her attitude show no matter how much people bugged her, but she always had trouble taking that advice to heart. And her father has been gone a long, long time.

"That's fine Mrs. Denari," says Sarah, in a dry monotone.

"Okay." Mrs. Denari smiles. What teeth she has to show are yellow. "How about three for eight then?"

"That's alright," says Sarah. The old woman once told her how her husband of forty years went out at night to get her cough medicine because she wasn't feeling well and was hit and killed by a city bus while crossing Seventh Ave with his walker. Sarah remembers that and tries to be patient. "You're always the good bargainer, you know."

Mrs. Denari waves her hand. "You're too sweet."

Sarah's cell phone vibrates in the pocket of her jeans. She pulls it to see who's calling and looks to the back of the store for her coworker. "Beatrice, can you come up front and check out Mrs. Denari, please? I have to step outside to take a phone call." She nods and waves goodbye to Mrs. Denari before pressing the green answer button on her phone screen and stepping out of the store onto the Brooklyn street. She leans her back against the neighboring brick building and puts the phone to her ear. "Hi Mom."

"I don't know why he never answers when I call him," says her mother, Barbara Bernauer. "He never returns my messages. I can't even remember the last time I even talked to him. Is it too much to ask? Why doesn't he want to talk to his own mother?"

Sarah can think of reasons. Not that they're justified. Barbara Bernauer did the best she could with the hand she was dealt.

"It's his own thing, Mom." A group of rowdy kids just out of school is walking near Sarah, singing and yelling, and she gets distracted. Some other people frown and shake their heads at the kids. Sarah smiles at them and makes sure they see it. "He'll come around," she says.

Barbara coughs into the phone. "But how long has it been, honey? I'm not going to live much longer. I hope he realizes that."

Sarah turns away from the street and faces the brick building she was leaning against. "Don't talk like that, Mom. Look, I'll try to talk to him and see what his issue is. He's just being a sour puss like he always is."

"Thank you sweetheart. Tell him I'm sorry and that I love him, would you?"

Sarah brushes a strand of her light brown hair from her face. "Mom, you don't have anything to be sorry for."

"I did the best I could for him. And for you too. I hope you know that."

"I know, Mom. I know." She pauses for a second and watches Mrs. Denari leave the store with a brown paper bag weighted down with what Sarah assumes must be a dozen dishes. "But look, I need to get back to the store now. Beatrice needs my help with some customers."

Hanging up, she realizes that she knows exactly why Brett has trouble talking to their mother, and to her too. Because sometimes it's too hard to face head-on the sadness of the people you care about the most.

When she comes back into the store Beatrice is folding a pair of Dockers on the front counter. There aren't any customers. "That poor lady, she just needs somebody to talk to," says Beatrice, in her thick Colombian accent.

Sarah looks at her with an upturned eyebrow.

Beatrice shakes her head. "Mrs. Denari, I'm talking about. The woman, her husband dies. Her kids are grown and can't be bothered. I think you and me are the closest thing she's got to friends."

Sarah looks down at her phone before putting it back into her pocket. "Yeah, I think you're right."

Beatrice puts aside the pants she's folded and takes another pair out of a white laundry basket. She holds them in her hands in front of her and assesses them for holes and stains, then looks over them at Sarah. "Everything okay?"

Sarah wipes the back of her hand across her eyes and then looks at it to make sure it isn't wet. "It's my mother. She's lonely in that house with all those memories. I'm the only person she has to talk to, I think. My asshole brother never returns her calls. Like he's got so much going on." Sarah shakes her head and picks a pair of pants out of the basket.

A customer walks in and Beatrice says hello. "That's a shame," she says to Sarah. "She still livin' in that town you grew up in, right?" Sarah nods. "What's the name of it?"

"Madison Park," Sarah says.

"It a nice town?"

Sarah adds the pants she's folded to the pile and takes out another. "On paper, I guess, but no, not really."

Beatrice's eyes follow the customer. He's a grey haired man with glasses that comes into the store once a week but never buys anything. "What do you mean it's nice on paper?"

"If you were to look it up online, like on some real-estate website, it'd probably tell you the property values

9

weren't bad and that the schools were okay. But there are some bad apples there for sure. There always have been."

Beatrice nods in understanding. "Is it part of all that heroin shit I hear in Jersey? It's everywhere right?"

"I guess so," says Sarah. "I mean, I don't pay attention to the place and I don't know much other than what my mother tells me, but I wouldn't be surprised and I wouldn't be surprised if some of the people I grew up with were involved. There's always been that element."

~ ~ ~

After work Sarah takes a subway to Saint Vitus, a small venue and bar at the other end of the borough. There's some punk band playing. They remind her of her brother – the other one.

The singer has red hair that's spiked high. He's got a ring in each nostril and two in each eyebrow. He swings the microphone stand and bangs it on the stage. He's wearing tight black jeans and a sleeveless black t-shirt. He jumps off of the bass drum and spits into the crowd. There are kids jumping around and running in circles.

It's 1AM when Sarah leaves.

The streets are empty – at least as empty as they get in Brooklyn. A cab or two go by. There are people mingling in front of bars, smoking cigarettes. There's a woman puking into the gutter and a guy standing behind her holding her hair back. It's about a five-block walk to the subway.

She turns off the main road and there are even fewer people, fewer lights. There's a shape coming towards her. It's staggering. Probably a drunk, she thinks. Still, she holds her bag to her chest and crosses to the other side. The person coming towards her crosses too. Sarah takes out her phone, but she keeps walking.

About ten feet before she gets to them, the person picks up into a run. Sarah's too late to react. She tries to turn but they're already pulling on her bag. She holds the bottom of it and turns her whole body. The strap rips, but she holds tight. She puts one leg behind the person and looks at them. It's a guy, skeleton skinny. Sarah pushes the bag into his chest and takes him to the ground over her leg. She puts all her weight onto her right leg and then brings the knee to his chest. She keeps doing it until he lets go of the purse.

"Goddam, bitch."

She stands up and kicks him in the face and says, "Do not fuck with me."

~ ~ ~

Walking up the steps in front of her apartment, still shaky from her altercation, Sarah feels her phone vibrate. Who would be calling her this late? She wonders as she takes it out and looks at the number. She recognizes the area code – the same as her mother's, but it's not her mother.

There is a man's voice when she answers. It's firm, authoritative, but still gentle. She thinks maybe it's a cop. She doesn't recognize the name. Then the voice says doctor. She hears some words about her mother and a fall and a stroke and then the word hospital, but they sound like they're coming from the other side of a long tunnel.

CHAPTER 3

Al is on his chest purring like a lawn mower when Brett wakes up. The sun has just started to rise and shards of light come through tree leaves and branches and into the cabin. Brett picks up his cell phone with one eye open and listens to one of his voice mails – the one from Fred telling him where he has to go for work.

He showers and puts on the same clothes he slept in. No one will notice, they never do. If anyone does, it's Fred and he'll never say anything. As long as Brett shows up where he's supposed to, Fred never sees anything wrong with what he does. He feeds Al, downs a protein shake, does a series of push-ups, and is out the door.

He pulls up at the house and waits for Fred. A woman opens the front door and looks at Brett. She's got blonde hair pulled into a ponytail and has a baby on her hip. Brett can feel her eyes on his scar. He nods at her and then closes his eyes and leans back on the headrest of his seat.

It's the same as always. She's expecting him to come to the door and introduce himself, explain what they're going to start first. He doesn't care. Fred can do the talking when he gets here, he thinks.

There are kids riding their bikes in the street. They're doing jumps off of the curbs. Brett watches them. He thinks they're brothers. One's bigger and better on the bike than the other. The smaller one is just trying to keep up, not complain, not raise the scorn of his cooler older brother.

Fred pulls up in his box truck and parks in front of Brett. There's ladders strapped to the top. Brett gets out and stands on the back bumper of the truck and starts to take them down.

"Well, good morning," Fred says. There's a new guy with him that gets out of the passenger seat. He's got a black baseball hat pulled down nearly to his eyebrows. He's young, in his early twenties. "This is Jay," says Fred. Jay nods and Brett nods back. "You say anything to the homeowners?"

Brett lifts a ladder up on his shoulder. "What do you think?"

Fred shakes his head. "I oughta go and do it."

Fred Donte is a thick and tall man in his mid-forties. Brett has worked for him for ten years, ever since he moved here from Jersey.

Brett has his work belt around his waist with a power drill and his hammer. He puts the ladder against the house and starts pulling nails out of siding. Within a few minutes he's torn down half of the front of the house and has worked up a sweat. Fred takes the other ladder and pulls down the rest. Jay works on the ground picking everything up. He works slow, doesn't say much, and smells like pot.

Brett works with his phone in his pocket. He feels it vibrating all day. When lunch rolls around he looks at, sees missed calls, mostly from his sister Sarah, and messages. He doesn't feel like being complained at again for not talking to his mother so he doesn't listen to them.

Fred eats his lunch next to Brett. Both of them sit on the curb. Jay is in the cab of the box truck that Fred drove, sleeping. He nods in his direction and says to Brett, "I don't know about this kid."

Brett doesn't have lunch. He's drinking from a plastic bottle of water. When he finishes it he crushes it in his hand and tosses it in the back of his truck. There are more kids running in the street now, two girls and three boys, shooting each other with squirt guns. Brett changes his focus from them to Jay. "Seems harmless to me."

Fred's eating a sandwich on a roll. Mustard is hanging

in his mustache. "He smells like pot. Shit, so much so that I'm afraid I'll get pulled over and ticketed for a DUI or something. Hell, smell my shirt." He lifts up his t-shirt and pushes it towards Brett.

"No thanks," he says, pulling his head back, "I'll take your word for it."

They sit silent for a minute. Fred chews and then he says, "I wish they were all like you."

Brett laughs and looks at Fred like he has two heads. "You must be outta your fucking mind."

"No way, man, I mean it. I mean, shit, you don't say too much and I think most of the customers think you're a serial killer, but I never once had a complaint about your work. Hell, you know that."

Brett stands from the curb and puts his hands in his pockets, looks at the ground. "You're an easy man to work for, what can I say."

Fred stands too. He's trying to look Brett in the eyes, but Brett's resisting. "Jesus, kid, learn how to take a compliment, would you."

Brett starts to walk back towards the house. They have the back of the place to pull the siding off of now. "Guess I need more experience getting them."

~ ~ ~

Brett goes home after work and Al greets him again. He takes a top round cut of steak out of the freezer and fries it. He cuts off some narrow pieces and puts them in Al's bowl.

When Brett drives to the Towne Diner in Scranton to meet Nate, he blasts music and pounds the steering wheel like a drum. The CD in is one of the first he ever owned. It's a soundtrack from a movie made in the 90's, some dark revenge thriller.

Nate's already sitting in the diner when Brett gets there. He's a black guy in a white place; 6, 2' and not an ounce less than two hundred and fifty pounds. His shoulders are about as wide as the front of Brett's truck.

He's at a booth in the back of the diner, talking to the owner, Sal, and a waitress whose name Brett can never remember. They're asking Nate about cars, which one's he'd recommend, how to fix simple problems like loose hoses, and the general difference between cars made now and cars made 40 years ago. Everybody likes Nate; he's always got something to say.

Brett nods at Sal and the waitress as he sits down across from Nate. "What d'ya want, honey?" the waitress asks.

Brett picks the menu up off the table and hands it to her. "Ten ounce steak, medium rare, baked potato."

Nate laughs. "Shit, you are a creature of habit, my friend." He looks at Sal. "This guy has ordered the same damn thing here I think every time we've come."

Sal laughs. "Hey, that's okay. Nothing wrong with a guy who knows what he wants."

When Sal and the waitress leave, Nate loses his smile and leans across the table. "I got a call from Jeanine. Remember that women, three kids, lived out of a bunch of motels in Stroudsburg, had the cigarette burns on her chest?"

Brett nods.

"Well, like I said, Jeanine had a call. The five year old called 911. When she got there the woman was dead, in the bathroom. The floor was wet. It looks like she could have slipped on the floor and hit her head on the sink."

"Is that what actually happened?"

"How should I know man?"

"Anybody talk to the guy?"

"Well, here's the thing, nobody can find the son of a bitch."

"Fuck."

"That's what I said. Little coincidence he split right when she falls and hits her head."

"Just a little."

"Yeah, but you know man, we can't do it all. Some fall through. Just think of all the people we've helped. That's what I do, when I hear some news like that."

"Let's find him."

"No, we've got other stuff to do."

"Oh yeah?"

"Oh yeah."

CHAPTER 4

Madison Park, New Jersey, has been around since the 1920's. It was mostly farmland when it was first incorporated for the purposes of pooling resources and creating public schools and a police force. About in the middle of the state, slightly closer to New York than Philadelphia, it's along a main thoroughfare. The Turnpike, the Parkway - all the roads that people outside New Jersey think the whole place is made up of - run through it. It was one of the first towns to have more than one train station. Some families there in the 20's still have descendants in the town.

In the 50's and 60's factories came because of all the available land and the proximity to major markets. The suburbs came with them so all the workers had places to live. The auto-industry came; there were a number of auto-plants built in the southern part of the town. It never grew to rival Detroit or even Flint, but there were enough jobs to draw people in. There was an air-conditioning factory, a place that made cosmetics, a gasoline refinery, and chemical plants.

The population boomed to over a hundred thousand people in the 70's. People of every background and national origin moved in. It wasn't just a place for the working class either. Plenty of upwardly mobile professional-types came too and took public transportation to the cities. The old families stayed around. Those that didn't work in the factories got jobs with the police or the fire department.

Beginning in the mid-'80s and continuing into the 2000s, the industrial-base crumbled. Every single factory closed. Either it was shuttered and abandoned or knocked to the ground and converted to retail space. It used to be that when a kid graduated high school they had three options: go off to college; become a cop or a fire fighter if you were lucky enough to be related to somebody that would hook you up; or get a job in one of the factories making something. It wasn't glamorous work, the factories, but they paid enough to support a family.

When the factories closed some of the families moved out. Some people got jobs at the retail places. The people that commuted to the cities, the recent arrivals, they were fine. It was the long-standing inhabitants, the people with the roots that got hurt. Unemployment brought poverty and poverty brought alcohol and drug abuse.

Now, there's a blighted section along Route One that stretches onto the side streets for a few miles. What's open there are only the adult bookstores and the motels. There's a few big box stores that are doing well a little further north.

The center of the area was once a Ford plant. There are warehouses on neighboring streets, closed as well, covered with graffiti and the windows are boarded up. There used to be pizza places and bars, but they've mostly crumbled to the ground now or have been overtaken by weeds to the point where nobody can tell what they once were.

The whole town isn't like this neighborhood, but to some people this neighborhood is the world they know and they never step out of it.

There's a man in a grey tracksuit leaning against a fence that borders the old plant. Some of his gut is hanging out in front of him. Grass surrounding him is as high as his knees. He has his hood up and his hands in the front pouch of his sweatshirt. He looks at every car that drives by. The road isn't as busy as it once was, so every passerby might be a customer. There's a friend of his lying on the ground next to him with a piece of cardboard covering his face.

A blue Trans-Am pulls up, making a squealing sound,

and grayish blue smoke billows from the exhaust. A skinny older man gets out. The door creaks as he does, looks like it'll fall to the ground it's hanging over so much. The man's got to be in his fifties at least, but who knows? Heroine ages you. His eyes are sunken. He has a gut, but his arms and legs are gaunt. There's a woman behind the wheel with frizzled brown hair and sloppy red lipstick. Eyeliner is streaked down her face. Her head is bouncing back and forth like she keeps falling asleep at the wheel and then catching herself.

The man with the sunken eyes walks over to Shane and holds out a wrinkled twenty. Shane hands him a bag and takes the money.

"This is all I got for now, bro." Shane shrugs.

He looks at the twenty before he pockets it and notices wet blood on the edge of it, so he reaches out and wipes it off on the front of the man's shirt.

"Fuckin' gross, yo. Clean your shit up before you come buying."

The man doesn't notice Shane rubbing the money on him.

"When you gonna get some more?"

"Not sure. Next week maybe." Shane looks at the bill again and stuffs it into his pocket as he shakes his head.

"That ain't no fucking good, man." The man turns to the woman in the car and shouts, "He ain't gonna get no more till next fucking week."

The woman leans over in the car. She's lit a cigarette and it's hanging from her lips, about to fall and set the car on fire.

"Fuck him." Her voice sounds like she gargles glass and rusty nails.

Shane flips the woman the bird and grabs his crotch at her.   "Go on over to Perth Amboy," Shane says to the man. "They've got plenty. All the shit you need. And control that fucking bitch of yours"

"Calm down," says the man, "she ain't mine, just some bitch."

"Whatever," says Shane.

The man is clutching the bag of heroin in his hand. "I don't like dealing with them spics over in Amboy."

Shane steps back to lean against the fence again. He looks down at his friend on the ground who hasn't moved or shown any sign that he hears the conversation around him.

"Well then I guess you're just gonna have to wait, son."

"Son? I could be your fucking father you little prick."

"But look who's coming to who," says Shane. He gestures outward with his hands like he's going to attack and the man flinches. "Now get outta here before I take my shit and your money."

The man grunts something indecipherable and goes back to the car. The woman inside is scowling at Shane. He gives her the finger again.

A half an hour later and another car comes down the road. Shane knows who it is. Not a customer. He looks down again. "Fuckin' Acardi, yo. Man always busting my balls." There's no reaction from his friend with the cardboard on his face.

The car is a black Crown Victoria with tinted windows. He walks to the curb before it gets to him. The passenger-side window rolls down and Shane leans in. Cigar smoke comes out at him.

"Shit, bro."

Norman Acardi says to him, "Give me what you got." Norman isn't as fat as Shane, but he's still got a layer of it. His is over muscle. His hair is greased back and he's covered in pockmarks.

"What're you talkin about, bro, shit, don't I need some for myself?"

"Give it to me, and I'll take care of you, later. You know that."

Norman talks to Shane like he's talking to a toddler – slow and clearly enunciating every syllable – but one he's about to smash with brass knuckles – something that he actually has stuffed in his pants pocket at all times.

"Nah, bro. I'll give you your split, like we agreed."

Norman closes his eyes and takes a deep breath. He motions for Shane to bend further into the car. When Shane does, Norman says, "Do you remember Ray?"

"Course I do."

"Do you remember what happened to him? Rodney told you, right?"

Shane looks at the seat of the car and shakes his head. "Can't forget." Then fear comes over his face as he makes the connection.

Norman smiles. "Give me what you have. Besides, you're not starving."

Shane shakes his head. "Shit." He reaches into his pants pocket and pulls out a fat wad of cash.

Norman grabs it. "I should get you more H on Friday. Tell your people to hold their shit."

Shane steps away from the curb.

"Yo, I'm tryin'. Can't we get some from somebody else? Always gotta deal with the Mexicans?"

Norman cocks his head. "You and Rodney with that shit. You want to be the one to tell them were dealing with somebody else?" Shane shakes his head. "I didn't think so. And again, don't make me remind you about your friend Ray."

~ ~ ~

Officer Dan Nichols drives a patrol car. It's his zone, for now anyway. They're always changing it. The chief's got something against him, he thinks, believes it's because he doesn't come from a family of cops like so many of the other guys. He sees a fat man standing against a fence by the old Ford plant. He knows who it is by the shape, like a manatee standing upright.

"What are you doing Shane?" he says, out of his window. "You think I don't know what goes on here."

"I think you don't know shit."

Dan parks and gets out. He runs over to Shane, grabs him by the shoulders, spins him around, and pushes him against the fence. He's pulling one hand behind Shane's back, about to make his shoulder pop, and has his other forearm against the side of Shane's face.

"Shit's still police brutality," says Shane. A wire from the fence digs into his lip.

Dan holds Shane against the fence and pats him down with his other hand, emptying his pockets. When he finds nothing he pushes Shane one more time against the fence with both hands, hard.

"You're a disgrace. Mom's got all these pictures of you around, you know that? She talks to her nurses about you. I should tell her the truth, you piece of trash." He looks on the ground, next to Shane, and sees Chino lying in the deep grass, with the broken box covering his face. "Who the hell is that?"

"Chino, you remember him?"

"Yeah," Dan says. "What's he doing?"

"Motherfucker's takin' a nap."

Dan kicks Chino in the side.

"Get up, Chino."

Chino doesn't respond. Dan pushes the cardboard off his face. Chino is bloated and purple. There's frothy sputum around his mouth.

"Jesus Christ, Shane." Dan bends down, checks to see if he's breathing and then grabs his hand to check his pulse. "Jesus Christ Shane. He's fucking dead."

~ ~ ~

Dan clocks out at the end of his shift and goes to his own car in the department parking lot. There are other officers mingling, but he just waves at them and keeps on walking. Officer Pete Waxman is pulling up in his personal vehicle for the nightshift.

"What's going on, Danny Boy," he says, stopping next to him.

Dan throws up his hands, flustered. "Another day in paradise."

"Tell me about it," says Waxman.

"I'd think you'd rather me not."

"Well if that's the case then you probably should."

"Found a dead kid today."

"Just another day in the park."

"He was with my brother. He hung around us when we were kids. I remember him on training wheels."

Waxman makes a whooshing exhale sound and shakes his head, takes his sunglasses off and looks at Dan in the eyes.

"Now I find him dead on the ground with track scars up and down his arms. God, I know his mother. She still lives in town."

"You gonna be the one to tell her?"

"Nope."

Pete spits out of his car window onto the asphalt. "Well, then there are things to be thankful for after all."

"I guess so, but I'll tell you, sometimes it doesn't feel like it. Not here. I mean look around. This place is falling apart."

"I know."

"Where are the jobs? Everyone I grew up with is either dead or in jail or on dope."

"Everyone?"

"Well, I suppose that's an exaggeration, but damn near everyone. And what about the next generation, the kids coming up now?"

"They better get the hell out. That's my plan," says Waxman. "Ten more years on the force man. Ten more years. Hell, maybe I'll get a promotion in that time, bring in some more in my pension. Then I take it and move down to the Carolinas. This state is too expensive. And look what you get for it."

"Trust me, I know."

"Yeah man, you have the girls. I don't know how you do it, on your own and everything. But listen to me, alright, you've got a good head on your shoulders, alright, more than any of these other bozos on this department, and you should do something with it, you understand what I'm saying."

"Like what?"

"Genero's retiring. Run for the union pres position."

"And what good would that do? I'd run a bunch of fundraisers."

"No man," says Waxman. He pats his hand on the car door. "You stop that nonsense, or maybe you keep the fundraisers, but you have them go to things that matter, drug prevention programs, shit like that."

"You think that will work? Instead of going to pay for defense for guys like Jones and Mitchels?"

"The hell with those guys. You and I and everybody else knows there's things in that story of theirs that don't line up. You mean to tell me that these little Indian guys were a threat to them? C'mon. We need to end this nonsense. People in this town don't respect this police department, like we're a mafia. That's how they see us."

"Well since you've got it all together, why don't you run for it?"

"Because I've been around too long. All the guys with the history around here've got my number already."

"And they don't have mine?" says Dan.

CHAPTER 5

Norman Acardi pulls into the parking lot of Harold's restaurant on the boarder of Madison Park and Iselin. It's a restaurant that specializes in over-sized comfort food. There's a freezer on the wall near the entrance with giant cakes and éclairs the size of Norman's head. The waitresses, the hostess, the owner, everybody, knows Norman and says hello. It's like he's the mayor, but actually, in Madison Park, someone like Norman Acardi has more power than the mayor.

He used to go to the place with his father — tagging along to union meetings. He was like the department mascot. His father went from a beat to detective to union president and after ten years of that he became chief. Then he had a heart attack and died with his face in one of those giant éclairs and coffee spilled all over his lap.

Norman planned a similar trajectory. Similar, but better. No worrying about money for him. His father cared about making the right impression, about caring what people in town thought about the department, about community relations. None of that shit, Norman thought. They were safe, weren't they, and that's all that mattered. So what if he got a little extra. If people knew everything, they'd be fine with it. Of course.

The hostess tells him to follow her and he does, watches her ass as she walks. They pass tables. Norman glances at them. They're all piles of filth, all the people. So fat they have to pull their chairs out, like that Shane piece of shit.

Like all other restaurants in the state, there's no smoking at Harold's, but when the hostess opens the door to the back room it's filled with guys either with cigars or cigarettes. They cheer when Norman comes in. There's four tables all lined up in one row. At the center of the table are Jones and Mitchel. Dumb fucks, is what Norman thinks of them. If you're gonna beat somebody up, do it till they're dead so nobody can talk. Not that it matters. They'll be fine.

Coming up to meet him is the chief, Lou Genero. Lou's grey hair is slicked back the same way Norman's is. In fact, it was Lou who showed Norman how to comb his hair. Back when Lou was a rookie and Norman was a kid, he'd come over for Sunday dinner. He'd throw a baseball around with Norman and then Lou and his father would talk shop or politics or whatever.

Lou took the union president job too. He's had it for fifteen years now. Most people would think that one person can't be both the chief of police as well as the president of the police union, but there's a thing about rules in Madison Park that most people don't realize: they don't matter. But the old bastard can't cut either position anymore. Can't cut work at all. He shakes too much. People have asked him about Parkinson's but he dismisses with a shake of his jittery hand every time.

He takes Norman by both shoulders. "There's the guy I'm talking about."

Rodney Ariosto walks up. "What's going on, Buddy?" He's one piece of muscle with colored sleeve tattoos. Norman thinks he looks like he's a criminal and he is. He works with Norman on and off the force. "Heard some kid died over by the plant. Overdose," says Rodney. "It was over the radio."

"Jesus H. Christ," says Lou. "That stuff is everywhere."

"Yeah, I heard," says Norman. "You gonna keep that outta the papers, Rodney?"

"Nobody'll know."

Lou smiles. "That's right. We don't need people thinking the wrong thing about this town now. You boys can deal with it the way we always did. Just us."

"That's right old man," says Norman, "just like the old days." He looks at Rodney and winks. Then he motions with his head over to Jones and Mitchel who are laughing and drinking. "How are they holding up?"

"How's it look like they're holding up?" says Rodney. "They're doing fine."

Norman takes out a roll of bills. They're neater now than when Shane gave them to him. He separates the bills. He gives half to Lou and says, "This is for the dinner." The he gives the other half to Rodney and says, "This is for the defense."

"Thank you, my boy," says Lou. Then he puts his arm around Norman. "We've been talking around the table. Everybody seems to think you're a good fit for president. Once I'm off. Just two weeks. So what do you say, Normy?"

Rodney laughs. "Ha, the new union president. I knew it would be him."

Norman nods. "Sure, I'm in. Gotta run, right?"

"Gotta run," Rodney says, and laughs again. "This guy's a real fucking comedian."

Norman knows it's an act with Rodney. The guy's got his nose so far up his ass lately he can feel him in his intestines. Rodney was there when Ray died, even helped dispose of the body. Norman had reasons to get rid of Ray, but chose to do it with Rodney around to send the message that he was in charge and if he was crossed there would be costs. The Mexicans in Philly were who they dealt with and who they'd always deal with as far as Norman was concerned. It was the long game. The Mexicans had the most guys, the most reliable supply over time, and the widest national and international connections, and the most likely to come down hard if a group of their distributors was working with somebody else. That relationship had to be managed. If things came a little slow from time to time, so what. To Norman, anyone that didn't see it his way or at the very least didn't tow the line regardless of how they felt, needed to be handled.

Ray was one such person. He'd been getting his own supply of H and other things; pills, cocaine, crystal, from Perth Amboy. Norman had a suspicion something was going on. His crew was selling less. Shane had supply left over at the end of the week. Bobby and Joe and even Joe's little brother, Kenny, the pussy - all Norman's old friends from childhood - were ratting on Ray. Bobby always had a particular allegiance to Norman and he was the first to squeal, said he was in the car with Ray when he went to Perth Amboy. He left Bobby in the car and went in to some boarded up house on Smith Street, wouldn't say what he was up to. Bobby told Norman right then that he thought something was going on. Norman couldn't believe how stupid Ray could be thinking Bobby wouldn't rat. The guy told Norman everything, practically told him when he took a shit. Joe and Kenny corroborated the suspicion, said Ray had more cash than normal.

So Norman, convinced by Bobby and Joe that he should at least shake Ray down, decided to investigate a little. With Rodney, he tracked Ray down, in a squad car no less, brought him to the boat docks at the edge of the Raritan River and made him empty his pockets. There were bags with all sorts of shit, shit the Mexicans didn't supply, and wads of cash.

Norman told Rodney in the car that he'd just rough Ray up, teach him not to go around, to follow orders, but that's not what happened. Norman threw the first punch and Ray fought back. He dodged it and kicked Norman in the stomach. Norman had enough. He reached into his pocket and slipped on the brass knuckles. After he landed the first punch with the metal on his hand it was over. He beat Ray's brains to pulp.

Norman pushed the body into the water and then Rodney helped him clean up. From that time on, Rodney had been a little different around Norman, a little less inclined to talk back.

He knew the bastard still harbored ambitions. It was the way the guy carried himself. He paid too much attention for somebody content being a partner or an underling. For the time being, fear had to work. Norman wasn't quite ready to deal with killing a fellow officer and all the hassle it would bring. But let Rodney try something, Norman had thought, he'll end up in a watery grave just like Ray.

Genaro walks away from Rodney and Norman. Rodney watches him and shakes his head. "The guy should've retired long ago. You want the chief spot too?"

Norman snorts and puts both of his hands on his belt, pretends to adjust his pants. "I don't think so. You want it?"

Rodney raises both hands. "No sir. I was just asking. You could do it, you know. The guys would love it. The mayor knows you well enough to appoint you. Have you spoken to him about it?"

Just keep digging your nose further up my ass, Norman thinks. "No, I haven't. To tell you the truth, Rod, I'm not too interested in being the chief. Too much work there." He smiles to act like he's joking, but he isn't. "The mayor'll appoint somebody like that Waxman guy. And let him, for all I care. It'll create a nice veneer."

"Fuckin' Waxman," says Rodney, "he and that fucking Nichols act like they're Boy Scouts."

CHAPTER 6

September 1990

Brett was lying in bed, dreading the day. The summer wasn't great, but an awful summer was still better than the first day of school. His room at their house in Madison Park was the smallest in the house. The windowsill had wrestling and karate trophies on it and the walls were covered in posters — no bands or super heroes, but fighters, Olympic wrestlers, Bruce Lee, Joe Lewis, and others. There was a diagram of the human body that had markers on every pressure point.

His father, Joseph, came in, fixing his tie. "There's my tough guy," he said. "First day of the seventh grade."

Brett grunted and rolled over.

He sat down on the bed next to Brett. "Listen, I know you're upset about karate class, okay. I know how much you like it. Once I find some work maybe we'll be able to afford it again."

Brett opened one eye and looked at his father, whose tie was blue over a white button down shirt. "Where are you going?"

"I'm going to some interviews, hopefully something will pan out." He paused and patted Brett on the foot. "Time to start moving in a few minutes, alright?"

"Alright," said Brett, but he didn't move. He watched his father leave the room and then rolled over again.

Resting there, with his head against the sheetrock wall, he could hear his parents talking downstairs. They were in the kitchen, both of them getting ready in a hurry.

Brett knew she wasn't talking about him. He didn't

hang out with anyone. Well, he hung out with Dan, sometimes, but they loved Dan. She was talking about Brett's brother Jonathan.

"I don't know what you want me to do," his father said.

His mother slammed some dishes in the sink. "Talk to him, tell him you're worried. I tell him I'm worried all the time and he doesn't care. Maybe it will be different coming from you."

His father opened a closet door where they kept all the coats. It was old and falling apart, like everything else in their house, so it creaked. "At the moment, I think I have some other things to worry about. Don't you think? Like how I'm going to pay for all of us to live. And plus, isn't that kid's father a cop? How much trouble can they get in?"

Brett rolled his eyes.

"We can talk about this more when we both get home," Barbara said, "You don't want to miss your train." Then she called upstairs, "Jonathan, we're both leaving. Make sure your brother and sister leave on time. And don't miss the bus."

Jonathan muttered something from somewhere.

Then Brett's door opened and Jonathan was standing there. He had black hair, spiked like he had stuck his fingers in a socket. He had on a torn black shirt and torn jeans and a leather jacket. "Get up, you turd."

Brett stood up from the bed and rubbed his hands on his face. His red hair wasn't standing up as much as his brother's, but it still stuck up on one side. When he went into the bathroom he ran water into his hands and patted it down. There wasn't time to shower. He was too worried about being late.

He came out of the bathroom. Both their parents were gone. Jonathan was running up and down the stairs with Sarah, nine at the time, on his back. She'd always been a bit on the chubby side, but Jonathan was strong and liked to show it off. She was screeching and laughing, her hair in a ponytail, flopping up and down as Jonathan bounced on the steps.

"We need to go soon, Sarah," said Brett. "Mom will kill us if we're late."

Jonathan ran with Sarah on his back into the living room. The whole house shook with his deliberately heavy steps. He was stomping like a monster and roaring like one too. He stopped in front of the couch and grabbed Sarah's leg with both hands and then flung her onto the couch like she was nothing. Sarah screamed in terror while she was in the air, but giggled loudly once she was on the couch.

"Listen, turd," said Jonathan, "I'm gonna be out late, alright." Whenever Jonathan spoke his lip curled up. It was like Elvis, or maybe Sid Viscous. Brett thought it was deliberate, like how his brother said country and emphasized the first syllable so the word came out as cunt-tree.

Brett shrugged, "Alright."

Jonathan sat on top of their little sister. "Mom and Dad'll be worried, but just so you know, I'm not dead."

"I'm gonna tell them!" said Sarah, from underneath him. Her face was red.

Jonathan stood and turned around and rubbed his hand on her hair making strands stick out from the ponytail. "Ah, you're not gonna say anything, you butthead."

She made a raspberry with her lips that sprayed spit in every direction.

Brett had his book bag on his shoulders. "Who are you going out with?"

Jonathan rolled his eyes. "Oh gimme a break, what are you Mom?"

"No," said Brett, "but c'mon, if you're gonna tell me you should tell me who you're gonna go out with."

"Fine, fine," said Jonathan, "Norman and Bobby and Joe."

"Mom and Dad don't like them you know."

Sarah ran off upstairs to her room to get her things for school.

Jonathan lost his joking demeanor. "I really don't give a shit." Then he held up two fists and spread his legs. "What are you gonna do?" And then he smiled again and tapped Brett on the shoulder with his fist and pretended to kick him in the shin with his Doc Martin. "I gotta go catch the bus, turd. Make sure she gets to school in one piece, alright?"

"Alright," said Brett.

Jonathan shouted up the stairs at Sarah, like his mother had done to him only minutes before. "I gotta go, butthead."

Sarah ran to the top of the stairs. "Bye, asshole," she said, and then ran back into her room, laughing.

Brett and Jonathan were hysterical.

Brett walked his sister to her school, which was down the road from his. They walked without saying much. He knew she didn't think he was as fun as Jonathan. The words were never easy to flow between the two of them, not like they seemed to be between Jonathan and anyone else. His brother always had something to say; the same wasn't true for Brett. But Brett knew that he loved his sister and knew she loved him. When he was sick she would put blankets on him and get him JELLO their mom had made from the fridge. When she had a scraped knee he was the one to take her to get washed up. He was the quieter and softer brother and he was fine with that.

Jennifer Kyle, a girl Brett went to school with, walked past them and Brett turned his head as she walked. She was wearing a skirt and looked tan from summer vacation. There was some sort of glitter in her hair. Brett missed a bump in the pavement and lost his balance for a second.

"Oooh," said Sarah, "you like her. I'm telling."

His face turned almost as red as his hair. "Shut up."

Then Sarah looked up at him and smiled. "It's okay, Brett. I won't really tell anyone."

Brett looked at the ground and told her thank you.

Then Brett's friend Dan spotted them from down the street and caught up. They'd known Dan and his family, the Nichols's, for years. Such good people, Brett and Sarah always heard their mother say about them. "What's up guys," he said. "Hey Brett, why haven't you been at karate class?"

Sarah looked at Brett again and again Brett avoided eye contact with anyone.

"Oh," Brett said, "I didn't want to go. I don't like it anymore."

"Really?" said Dan. "I thought you loved it."

Brett shook his head. "Nah."

They got to Sarah's school. "See you after school," she said and she ran off to join her friends.

Brett and Dan walked on. In some ways Brett was jealous of Dan. He did everything so well without seeming to try. When they played baseball the kid hit the ball every time he was up. Brett had never seen him strike out. And he was fast too – the king of stealing bases. The teachers loved him and always picked him to clean the chalkboard; smiled whenever he answered a question and doted over his Halloween costumes every year. But Brett couldn't be too angry with Dan no matter how envious he was of him because Dan always talked to him. He wasn't the type who'd ditch his old friends for a new crowd the way so many kids did when they reached adolescence. When they got to their school there were a number of kids waiting outside for the front doors to open.

Kenny saw them and came over. Kenny had a mullet and torn blue jeans and a black book bag with a Marlboro cigarette logo on it. He smelled like Marlboros too. "Hey

Brett," he said, "my older brother has tons of beer and whiskey. He's gonna drink it after school with your brother and Bobby."

"So," said Brett.

Dan took a step back.

"They drink on top of the shopping plaza down the road. Norman will be with them so if they get caught it won't matter." He laughed and his teeth were yellow.

Brett and Kenny were different on many levels – Kenny was by far more aggressive than Brett and had even more difficulty in school and with making friends – but there were some understandings between them as younger brothers. They both got pushed around – though Kenny was pushed much more than Brett. The way Jonathan pushed Brett around was in a typical sibling manner. He'd call Brett names and punch him on the arm and one time hung him on a doorknob by his underwear, though he also hugged him and told him he needed to defend himself but that if he couldn't as his older brother he would be there to help out. Brett sensed that the relationship between Joe and Kenny might have had some of the same things, but, for reasons he couldn't clearly articulate at the age of 12, he knew the two relationships were still fundamentally different.

He once saw Joe give a kid a bloody nose with a plastic baseball bat after calling Kenny a retard for dropping the ball during a pickup game, but then when he was done hitting that kid he went over to Kenny and wacked him right in the balls with the bat like he was swinging a golf club; told him he had to stop giving people reasons to call him a retard. That was when Brett and Kenny and Dan were in the third grade.

Dan was there that time too, but his little brother, Shane, wasn't. Dan never let Shane hang out with him and other kids his age. People always teased Shane for being heavy and instead of defending Shane he just told him to stay inside so nobody'd make fun of him.

But ever since the incident with Joe and the plastic bat, Brett had a swollen sense of pity for Kenny that grew every time he saw the kid come to school with another welt on his arm or bruise under his eye.

Despite the welts though, Kenny had a strong allegiance towards his older brother. Where Brett would roll his eyes when he heard of something delinquent his brother had done, Kenny would stick his chest out with pride over the same thing, like when Jonathan and Joe and Norman were caught drinking under the high school bleachers. He'd imitate the behavior too. He was the only kid in their middle school that had ever come to school with the smell of alcohol on his breath. Brett on the other hand agreed with his father that his brother was acting like an asshole.

~ ~ ~

When Brett and Sarah got home from school their father was on the couch. His tie was thrown over the back of it and his shirt was unbuttoned. On the TV across the room was a rerun of MASH, but Joseph wasn't paying much attention to it. His head was in his hands and his sleeves were rolled up.

He looked up at them. There was stubble on his face that wasn't there in the morning and it made him look a few years older because it came in grey. Brett saw red in his eyes like he'd been crying and he wasn't sure if Sarah noticed.

"There are two of my favorite people," he said. "How was your first day of school?"

"Fine," said Brett.

"Awful," said Sarah.

Brett watched as their father wiped his eyes. "Oh, I'm sure that's not the case. It couldn't have been that bad."

"I already have homework," said Sarah.

"Well you better get started on it then. Brett, how about

39

you?"

"Yeah, I have some," he said.

"You better go do it then and then when you're done come on out here and you can help me fix some loose floor boards."

When Brett finished he went and found his father who had at that point fallen asleep on the couch while watching TV. Brett stood in front of him for a second and watched him sleep. The look on the man's face was of pure exhaustion. His mouth was open and there was some drool around it. He was snoring loudly.

Rather than wake him up, because he wasn't sure what type of mood he would be in if he did, Brett sat on the floor with his back against the couch.

At five o'clock he put on the Ninja Turtles. He knew he was too old for it. Jonathan would pick on him if he caught him, but with Jonathan not home and Sarah doing whatever it was she did, Brett was free to be himself.

During one of the commercial breaks, his father stirred behind him and put his hand down on Brett's shoulder. "Hey there," he said, groggy, "thanks for coming to join me."

"I wanted to watch TV," said Brett.

His father turned to face the TV. "What are we watching?"

"Ninja Turtles."

"Okay. Which one is your favorite again?"

"I don't like them anymore. It's too young for me. I have nothing else to do."

"That's fine," his father said.

When the show was over, his father got up from the couch. "Time to fix that floor board. You still want to help?"

"Okay,"

They went downstairs into the basement to where his father had squares of plywood. The place was filled with old tools and everything was covered with dust. It had a strange smell that Brett liked. It made him feel comforted and he wasn't sure why.

His father got out a stepladder and stood it up. The veins on his arms stood out and his muscles tensed. Brett thought it would be cool if one day his arm looked the same way. "Here," he said, "you get up on the ladder and I'll hand you what you need."

Brett went midway up the ladder and waited.

"I'm going to hold the plywood," his father said. "You've got to do the nailing."

"Usually I hold things while you hammer them," said Brett.

His father handed him a hammer. "Yeah, well, you're older now."

When they finished the job his father put the step stool back against the wall as Brett held the hammer.

"You can keep that," his father said, "It's about time you had your own."

~ ~ ~

Brett was lying in his bed again with his head against the wall when he heard his parents arguing. Again it was about Jonathan. They were worried about where he was. He thought about going to tell them.

Brett didn't sleep at all that night because they argued the whole time. Eventually they called the police.

Jonathan never came home again.

CHAPTER 7

Despite the amount of death in Sarah's life she's spent little time in hospitals. There's a discomforting smell to them that makes her want to vomit. It's the combination of plastic and cleaners and shit.

When she gets to the floor where they say her mother is there's an Indian doctor with a clipboard. It's not the same doctor she spoke to on the phone. She doesn't catch his name either. She feels like she's going to pass out and he looks like he's speaking to her from inside a fish bowl. His lips are dried and cracked and for some reason that Sarah can't figure out they're the only thing she can focus on, like there's a magnifying glass up to his mouth.

Inside the hospital room, Barbara is intubated. There's a long plastic tube coming from her mouth that's hooked up to a machine. There's stiches on the side of her head. The doctor tells her she had a stroke and then fell and hit her head. A neighbor found her. No one's sure exactly how long she'd been lying on the kitchen floor, but the doctor tells her he thinks it was a while, more than five hours. Sarah puts her hand to her mouth to mask her gasp. Then the doctor says something about brain damage and uses the word extensive.

She isn't sure what to do or what to say. She can't stand still. She sticks her hand in her pocket and feels a Skittle she left in there. When she takes her hand out green has rubbed off on it. A nurse comes in and rubs a wet washcloth against her mother's mouth, around the tubing, and then takes one bag of fluid off of the pole next to her bed and replaces it with another.

The doctor and the nurse leave her with her mother

after they explain there isn't much they can do. The woman is a vegetable, Sarah thinks. It's a terrible thing to think about her own mother and she wishes the thought didn't creep into her head, but it did. She'd be better off dead.

There's machines next to the bed and they're going off with an annoying song of beeps and buzzes. Outside of the room she can hear a million more beeps and buzzes along with hushed voices. She walks over to her mother and feels her forehead. It doesn't feel like her mother's skin. The face of the woman lying there doesn't look like her mother's face. "Mom," she says, "I want you to be okay." There's no response and she has the feeling there never will be.

For three hours she sits in an uncomfortable chair next to the hospital bed. The nurse comes in when it gets dark out, after many of the other visitors on the floor have left, and offers Sarah a blanket. After taking it and wrapping it around herself as best she can, she decides she needs to get out of the hospital. The surrounding town is the last place she wants to be, but she can't sit around any longer and watch her mother die.

She gets a cab to her old house and spends a second inside looking at all the disarray. There's blood on the table, furniture moved everywhere, broken glass from a coffee mug on the floor, and blood on the kitchen table and floor. She grabs her mother's car keys from on top of a pile of magazines and gets out of there too.

They used to go to a nearby deli when she was growing up to get newspapers and coffee and junk food. It's the only place she can think of to go, but when she gets there the place is different. It's a 7-11 now.

Inside there's a large man in a flannel shirt and jeans and work boots standing at the magazine rack with an energy drink in his hand. His back is towards Sarah, but something about him frightens her. His hands are covered in dirt and grime. He has on a mesh baseball hat and his thick neck has hairs shooting off of it. Sarah puts her head down and walks quickly passed him to grab a cheese Danish. From the corner of her eye she sees him look up from his magazine and watch her go to the counter to pay.

Once she leaves the store she hears someone walking behind her in the parking lot. The man begins to speak as she fumbles for the keys in her pocket. She never looks at him but she knows who it is. "I didn't think I would see you back here," he says. He sounds almost happy about it. "After all that happened and the things you said. People still talk about that stuff. You should leave, you whore." As she lifts her head he's already walking back inside the store.

Driving fast from the parking lot, the Danish she put on the seat next to her falls on the floor and she doesn't notice. She's too focused on getting her hands to stop shaking.

Back in the driveway at her mother's home she fumbles for the Danish off of the floor. It's fallen out of its bag and has dirt on it. Some of the cream-colored cheese has fallen out. "Fucking hell, Sarah," she says, and rolls down the window. As she throws the food onto the driveway her phone vibrates. It's the same number as before; the hospital. The Indian doctor tells her that her mother has died. He says they're sorry, that they did the best they could. Sarah closes her eyes and says thank you. She clutches the phone so tightly she's surprised it doesn't snap.

Before she puts the car in reverse she makes a phone call.

CHAPTER 8

It's nearing 5:30, when Nate typically closes up shop. He's got to call Jeanine and tell her that he's going to take care of that guy tonight.

He's never really believed in justice, either the justice system or in the idea that he can carry it out himself like some sort of comic book vigilante. No, for Nate it's about making sure people aren't abused, aren't raped, and aren't murdered. It's about making sure that fathers don't have to explain to their kids that their mothers won't be coming home.

It worries him, the thought of all the damage being done in the world, and that worry has made him who he is. It ruined his marriage. He held it together for ten years, but eventually all the questions he'd ask and the snooping – done because he was afraid for her, he told her and himself – broke it apart.

"But you can't stop everybody from getting hurt," his wife, Cynthia, said on many occasions, though Nate never agreed.

He cleans up his tools, wrenches of different sizes, wipes them with a rag and puts them in a large metal box against the wall. There isn't a single chip of paint on the box and no dents. The tools are like new, not because they aren't put through hell, but because Nate spent good money on them and doesn't want to spend good money on any more.

In the center of the garage is the auto lift he bought with what was left of the bank loan after he renovated the building. There's room for more than one lift, but it's good enough for now. Nate doesn't get enough business to justify purchasing another. On the ground next to the lift is his pipe wrench. It's red like the toolbox and as clean as everything else. It's about as long as his forearm. He wipes it with his rag and holds it in both of his fists like a baseball bat. Exhaling out his nose, he swings it back and forth. No, he thinks, he likes the tool but he doesn't need it to get his point across to people. He does just fine with his hands.

There's no answer when he calls Jeanine. "That woman never answers her phone," he mutters to himself before she calls back and his phone rings. "You screening calls?" he says.

"No, not at all," she says. "I was just napping. I've had a busy couple of days, like I explained before." Jeanine has a deep voice for a woman and has a build that matches it. Despite being about a foot shorter she's just as wide as Nate and nearly as strong.

"I don't mean to bother you. I wanted to call and tell you I was going to handle that teacher you told me about last week, alright. I've got a plan and everything."

Jeanine yawns into the phone. "Don't get hurt, you hear me. I need to bring in my car." Jeanine owns a 1986 Ford Mustang with 180,000 miles on it. She always brings it to Nate. It's the reason they met. He's replaced the transmission twice already.

Nate laughs. "You've got to get a new set of wheels, lady. What's going on now?"

"I don't think it's anything major. It stalls when I start it. I think maybe it's just a loose hose." She pauses, and says, "Does this plan of yours involve a certain redhead?" she says.

"Can't do this myself. You know that. What if the guy's got a weapon?"

"Oh, I know. I'd rather you be safe. Who else would fix my car? I'm just never so sure about him. He seems like he could lose it. You've got the right attitude about it. You know how to walk the fine line, but I don't know that he does. I'm always afraid that he could get you into something serious that you won't know how to get yourself out of."

Nate rolls his eyes. "I'm a big boy, Mom."

CHAPTER 9

Nate and Brett are scheduled to meet in the parking lot of a Wal-Mart off of route 80 in northeastern Pennsylvania. Wal-Mart is the only place Brett can afford to shop, so before Nate gets there he goes in to buy a t-shirt, but mostly to kill time, and to get away from his own thoughts.

Once, while waiting for Nate, he went into the Wal-Mart and looked at the guns. Generally, he stays away from guns. Fred's taken him for target shooting many times and he knows how to handle them, but he knows he's not the type of person that should own one, knows he'd get carried away.

After he gets the shirt, his plan is to go and sit in his truck and wallow in despair, as usual, but Nate pulls up.

Nate and Brett first became acquainted at the gym they both go to, the only one in a 25-mile radius around Brett's place, a radius that also encompasses Nate's auto shop.

When someone almost hit Brett with their car in the parking lot and he reacted by throwing an empty container of protein shake at them, Nate formally introduced himself and offered to buy him a drink. Brett declined the alcohol, but went and had a Coke. Nate explained himself then, said what he did and why he did it.

Nate grew up in Easton, Pennsylvania. His mom worked a night shift at a 24-hour diner and his father broke his back ten hours a day working in a cardboard box factory. One night his mother never came home. A few days later, somebody found her body in a dumpster. When Nate was in high school, his father spilled out that on top of having her throat cut she'd been raped, by two people.

In the car, Nate explains to Brett what the night's work is. "So I first hear about this from Jeanine," he says, "she gets this call for a girl – high-school girl – having difficulty breathing, at her home. She gets there and it turns out the girl is having a panic attack. Normally a bullshit call, right? But no, not this one. The mother insists that the girl go to the hospital. She says she's not acting like herself and hasn't been for some time."

"Jeanine, I mean you know Jeanine, she gets this really clingy vibe from the mother. The lady's high strung and Jeanine, hell, she knows that if she's gonna calm this girl down, she's just gotta get rid of the mother. So she tells the woman, yeah, she can come for the ride to the hospital in the ambulance, but she has to ride in the front with Jeanine's partner.

"In the back, Jeanine does what she does. She gets this girl some oxygen and sits across from her and holds her hand. She gets the girl to the point where she doesn't really need to go to the hospital, which if you ask me didn't need to happen in the first place, I mean, a panic attack."

"Who knows," says Brett.

"Anyway, the girl starts talking to Jeanine."

"Woman's got a super power."

"I swear, right? And just listen, man, wait until I finish, she got this out of this girl in the 20 minute ride to the hospital. Anyway, this girl is on the high school softball team, right. And she's close with another girl on the team, a friend of hers and our girl in the ambulance, she starts questioning her sexuality and all, I mean you see where this part is going, right?"

Brett nods.

"So the two girls kiss in the locker room sometimes after everybody else has left, and one time the coach, a dude, goes into the locker room and sees them. My question is what was the guy doing in the locker room in the first place, but whatever, it gets worse than that.

"One day the girl goes into his office. Now she didn't realize he'd seen them, so she wasn't thinking anything was up, but when she goes in there to talk about something, I don't know what, dude's sitting in his chair with is dick out."

Brett sits up. "Fuck."

"He says something like 'I know you like dirty shit so why don't you come here and do some of that dirty shit with me.' Our girl freaks and this guy says if she says anything to anybody he'll make sure everybody in the school knows she's a lesbian. This shit festers in the girl's head, like it would with anybody, I guess. The coach continues being a shit. He starts groping her if no one else is around, stuff like that. And then we have our present situation. She doesn't know what to do. She said to Jeanine she thought about taking some pills and killing herself. She saw no other way."

"I get that," said Brett.

"So do I, man. So do I."

"So, where's the coach?" asks Brett. "What's the plan?"

"Well, I mean, I heard this all from Jeanine about a week or so ago. I went to a softball game at the school, figured out who the coach was and I've been following him around."

"What do we know?"

"We know he lives in Scranton, alone. And we also know the guy frequents dive bars and strip joints. One place in particular he likes is called the Pleasuredome, which is where we're driving to right now."

Brett smiles. His feet are up on the dashboard. They're far out from the city now, surrounded by trees and darkness and some streetlights. "So what's the plan?"

"We wait until he comes out, follow him, stop him at the side of the road and deliver our message."

"How are we gonna stop him at the side of the road?"

"You see this clunker I'm driving, don't you?"

They pull up and the club is a windowless building with a white sign and positionable black letters that say "Pleasuredome."

Men come and go and they watch them. At other establishments in the same line of entertainment, there might be groups of guys going in together as part of a bachelor party or after-work engagement, laughing, dressed in business casual, but at the Pleasuredome it's only one guy at a time, wearing sweats or Dickies coveralls coated in grease. Some of the guys stumble, on the way out and the way in.

"That's him," Nate says, after they've been sitting there for an hour. "Place is only open one more hour. He's late tonight."

The guy is wearing a beige windbreaker and matching Dockers. His face is scarred from what must have been a terrible case of teenage acne and it looks like the surface of the moon, but with eyebrows. He's skinny in his arms and legs but has a gut.

"Now what's this guy's name?"

Nate laughs. "Oh shit, I can't believe I left that part out. My man's name is Steven Balder.

~ ~ ~

Balder comes back to his car. It's a beige Prius. He walks with the same tense gait he had on his way in. Even the strippers couldn't loosen him up.

Nate has dozed off in the driver's seat, but not Brett. He's watched the door of the place the whole time, never even took his phone out of his pocket. "Time to move," he says.

Balder drives past them and out of the parking lot. There are still a few people walking out of the place, dancers and bouncers. Nate opens his eyes and stretches his arms to the windshield.

Brett turns his head and watches through the windows

as Balder drives out of sight. "We have to go, man, our guy is gone."

"Relax," says Nate, "he's going home. I know the way he goes. Nowhere else open at this time, bro."

After five minutes on the highway they begin to follow him closely. Once it's only them and Balder on the road, Nate pulls up half a football field's distance behind him. Then closer. When he pumps the gas, the engine hums.

Balder slows down and pulls to the right. He sticks his hand out the window and waves for them to pass. They don't. "How long is this going to take?" Brett says. They can now see Balder looking at them in his rearview mirror and Brett raises a fist for him to see.

Balder speeds up. He keeps looking into the rearview mirror every couple of seconds. His eyes are red and he's screaming.

"He knows now," says Nate. He tightens his grip and looks at Brett. "Hold on," he says, and he straightens his leg, hard, jamming the pedal to the ground. Brett pushes against the dashboard and looks in front of him. When they hit Balder's bumper his tires screech and his car jolts forward. Nate and Brett bounce forward and backward in their seats, but both cars remain driving on the road. Nate does it again.

He pulls to the left, crossing the yellow line onto the opposite side of the road. He speeds up more so the nose of the car is halfway past the Prius's back left tire. Nate maintains the speed and looks to Brett for approval.

Brett grabs the plastic handle above his door. "Go for it."

He jerks the wheel to right and sparks fly. The collision makes a basketball-sized dent in Balder's car. Nate lightens up on the gas and they watch Balder careen to the left and then over-correct himself to right. He's back to the left and back to the right and then he's off the road, through a drainage ditch and into a tree. Nate kills the lights and stops the car on the side of the road, off onto the grass and dirt.

Brett takes his hammer from the back seat and Nate takes a tire iron from between the console and his seat. Balder's car is perpendicular to theirs. The windshield is shattered and the air bag has deployed. There's a hiss of steam coming from the hood.

Crouching and walking, Nate and Brett take to opposite sides, each of them careful not to make much noise. Brett taking the passenger side and Nate taking the driver's side. No communication needed, they move like a machine.

Before they reach him, Balder is out of the car. His face is covered in blood that can only just be seen in the dim headlights of his car. He's screaming and cursing.

"My God," he yells, with a cracking voice like an adolescent boy, "I told them I don't have the money. I'm a school teacher for Christ's sake." He's walking in their direction and shaking everywhere. There's something in his hand.

There's a series of loud pops. He's firing only in Nate's direction, but missing by miles. The bullets are hitting trees off in the distance. One manages to hit the front bumper of Nate's car.

Brett comes up behind Balder and hits him in the back of the knee with his hammer. It buckles his leg, but doesn't take him down. Balder shoots straight up into the air and then Brett grabs his hand. He twists it and pulls it behind his back, pushes the base of his thumb until it's even with the opposite side of his wrist. There's a few cracks and Balder drops the gun. He turns and swings, but Brett steps to the left and dodges it.

Nate comes and breaks his jaw with the tire iron. Teeth and blood fly in front of the beams from the broken headlights. Balder spins out of Brett's grasp and hits the dirt. He gets up to his hands and knees and starts to crawl away. Nate hurls the tire iron like a boomerang and it nails him in the ass, sending him face first into the ground.

Brett picks up the revolver Balder dropped, pushes out the chamber, and empties the bullets onto the ground. He scatters them with his foot. "Someone like you should not have a firearm, Mr. Balder." Then he tucks the gun in the back of his jeans.

"Shit," says Nate, in a pissed-off voice that Brett rarely hears, "motherfucker can't hit the side of a barn."

Balder is holding his face, moaning and rocking himself side to side. "I ron't hab da money! I ron't!"

Nate and Brett stand above him. "What the fuck is he talking about?" says Nate.

Brett crosses his arms and tilts his head. He wonders what went wrong in this man's life, but then it occurs to him, as it occurs to him every day, that something goes wrong in everyone's life. "Poor Mr. Balder thinks we're after him to collect a debt."

Nate picks up some dirt from the ground and throws it in Balder's face. "Damn, how many people did you piss off?"

Balder is sitting up now, sobbing, but he pauses to shrug his shoulders.

Brett feels a vibrating in his pants pocket and remembers he left his phone there. It goes on for a few seconds and then stops and starts again. He ignores it and looks down at Balder again. "We don't care about money, Mr. Balder. Whoever you owe money to, they're coming by to visit some other time. But that's not us. We're here to tell you, that somebody dumb enough to show his dick to high school girls is too dumb to teach high school girls. You understand?"

Balder looks up, dumbfounded. His face is swelling and turning purple.

"Look," says Nate, "you don't have to understand, alright. All you have to know is, tomorrow, you're going to go into the principal's office at your school and you're going to hand in your letter of resignation. Then you are going to find another place to live, preferably far away."

Brett interrupts. "And you are not going to teach ever again." Then he feels the phone vibrate one more time.

"That's right," says Nate. "Never the fuck again." He bends down into Balder's bloody face. "And if you do, or if we find out you've contacted that nice softball player, we will fuck up so much more than your car and your teeth."

Brett puts a hand on his head, as if he is about to rub his hair, and taps his fingers. "We'll kill you."

He and Nate look at each other and begin to walk to the car.

Balder calls out behind them, "How vo I get hum?"

Nate turns and says, "You think that's my problem?"

~ ~ ~

In the car on the way back to the Wal-Mart they talk about Balder.

"Who do you think he owes money to?" asks Brett.

"I don't know, but God damn, I started to feel bad for the guy. I almost gave him a ride home."

On the open highway with no other cars on the road, Brett opens the window. He takes out Balder's revolver, wipes it on his jacket, and then throws it off an overpass.

"Looked like a nice piece," says Nate.

Brett shakes his head and rolls the window back up. "I don't want it around."

~ ~ ~

In the early hours of the morning, Brett finally gets home and takes care of Al. Then he takes his phone out of his pocket to see what all the vibrating was about. There's four missed calls. All of them from his sister, whom he hasn't spoken to in half a year. Their last conversation ended with her calling him an asshole for not going home to see their mother more often. There's a voice message too.

He listens while drinking a Muscle Milk and taking a piss. Sarah's crying and her voice sounds like she's talking through gritted teeth.

"Why the fuck can you never answer your phone, Brett? Never, you know. Fuck, not even now." She's sniffling and it sounds so awful that Brett gets distracted and pisses on the floor. "But listen," she says, now sounding less angry and more like she's breathing heavy, about to hyperventilate, "Mom had a stroke today. She fell sorting mail at the kitchen table and hit her head. Brett, Mom is dead. Can you call me? Please, Brett. I'm back home."

CHAPTER 10

Bobby Reed is passed out on the couch that still smells like his grandmother even though she died ten years ago. If it wasn't for the house he inherited from her he would be out on his ass, so he doesn't mind the furniture even though it all has the same pastel floral pattern. But everything is faded and stained. The house was white, but now it's more of a grey from neglect. The wooden steps leading up to the front porch, the one's he and his friends used to bound up as kids, are cracked and sagging.

The couch isn't big enough for him, hasn't been since he was fifteen. His legs hang off the end of it. It's tough for him to get both shoulders on it. There used to be muscle on him too, but now he's just useless mass. He's lanky and flabby, with hands bigger than most people's faces. He's not as out of shape as Shane, but he's getting there.

His cell phone is on the floor, on the beer stained carpet, ringing, like it has been all morning. It's halfway under the couch, must have fallen that way when he collapsed. Not that he would remember. It's a flip phone and the ring tone is Crazy Train by Ozzy. He hears it in his dream and incorporates it, thinks he's at a concert. One eye opens, half way, and then he realizes that he's not at a concert, but still at his home, looking at his grandmother's piano that's covered in dust, cobwebs, and beer cans.

"What?" he says, when he answers, his speech still slurred from dreamland. He wipes drool from his face and realizes just how much his head is pounding. There are crumbs from something he doesn't remember eating stuck in his beard and he begins pulling them out and looking at them. The memory of going to 7-11 floats around somewhere in his brain.

"What the fuck is the matter with you? You can't answer the phone?" It's Norman. "Can you move that pick up to earlier?"

Bobby pushes himself upward and sits. The room is spinning around him. "The what?"

"Fucking think. Bad enough I've got to do this on the phone. I can't spell it out for you."

Bobby pauses. The room isn't spinning as much. "Nah, sorry, Norm. When they set a date they like to stick to it. That's what they said." Then he looks down at the floor. A thought pops into his head for the briefest of seconds. It says that there's something he has to tell Norman, but he can't remember what. Then the thought passes from his drug and alcohol addled brain.

Bobby has known Norman his whole life, though he can't state exactly why they're friends. Norman bullies him even has an adult. In fact, it's worse as an adult than when they were kids. But Norman helps with so much. It was Norman that hooked Bobby up with his current line of work and without that, yes, he would still have the house, but no money for food or way to keep the lights or the heat on. Norman is all Bobby has, so if there are some nasty words now and then Bobby supposes that's all right.

He's still thinking about his dream with Ozzy. Norman's yelling about something and it feels like the guy is coming through the phone with an icepick and sticking it in his ear.

"Are you listening to a fucking word I'm saying? Jesus Christ, I am fucking surrounded by morons" There's a pause, then, "Hell, Bobby, are you tapping into the supply again?"

Bobby sits straight up as if Norman is asking him the question in person. "Of course not," he says. Then the thought comes back, the one about him having to tell

Norman something. "Oh, hey, Norman." He pauses and stares at the wall, like it's going to tell him what to say.

"What?"

Bobby stares at the wall still. It feels like a train is slamming against the inside of his head, again and again. The words have escaped him.

"I'm gonna let you think," says Norman, "I've got work to do. If you remember what it is, give me a call."

"Wait," says Bobby, "I got it. You know who I saw back in town yesterday when I drove to the 7-11."

Bobby drives an old white van. He bought it because he wanted to start a plumbing business, but that, like many of his dreams, never materialized. Instead, he uses the van to do pick-ups for Norman. Most of the officers in town and in the surrounding area know not to stop it. After he does the pickup he splits the supply for distribution with Kenny, Shane, and Joe.

"Who, Bobby? Santa Claus?"

Bobby laughs. "No. Fucking Sarah Bernauer."

There is nothing on the other line for the first time in the conversation. Then, quietly, "That fuckin' cunt. God, remember all the trouble she caused? Shit."

"I just wanted to let you know," says Bobby, "but I figured, what's the big deal, right? I just didn't want you getting mad at me cause I didn't tell you." The silence made Bobby uncomfortable, made the train hit the inside of his head again. In a gentle voice, Bobby says, "You okay, Norm?"

Norman breaks his silence. "You did good, Bobby. Thank you for letting me know."

"But it's okay, right?"

"No, not really, I've got a lot going on right now, running for the union president position and all. I can't have her around bringing up the past, having people asking questions about it and that shit with her brother. And hell,

61

the shit with her other brother even. It would be good if she left as soon as possible." Norman then ends the conversation, says he'll come over at some point next week and help fix the front steps on his porch.

The room spins even faster when Bobby tries to stand up to go to the bathroom. He falls back down on the couch and it creaks under his weight. He pees a little on himself and rubs his hands on his face. A thought bounces inside of his head again, this one tells him that maybe he can do something to help Norman get rid of Sarah Bernauer.

CHAPTER 11

September 1990

The phone rang once. Joseph picked it up, must have been sitting next to it at the kitchen table. In the silence of the night the sharp ring made Brett shoot up in his bed.

"Who is it?" Barbara said, in a quiet but stressed voice that was like the ping of a taut rubber band. There was no answer, but the silence screamed. Both his parents were downstairs, he realized, meaning Jonathan still hadn't come home.

There was a window in the corner of Brett's room, and the dark sky outside it was getting lighter, making his trophies visible again. Someone on the street behind them started their truck. Birds started to chirp.

He thought his brother would be alright, that he would come home like he said he would, so throughout most of the night he worried about school, about fitting in, and he thought about Jennifer. When his father spoke in a tone he almost never heard, somber and low, it was as if those worries never existed and they were replaced by a sick feeling in his gut that was worse than anything he'd ever felt before, like the pieces of his stomach were tearing themselves apart.

The feeling was wrong, he thought, and he wanted to prove it to himself, so he got up from his bed and left his room, went to the top of the stairs where he could see down into the kitchen. But what he saw there made it worse. His father was still on the phone, the cord stretching to where he sat at the table, the whirls in it pulled straight. Tears were running down his face. His voice was trembling and thin.

This man that Brett thought was so strong, not invincible like when he was younger, but strong still, in this moment looked like wind could kill him. His hair was disheveled and his eyes were puffy.

At the other end of the table his mother stood, the chair pushed out behind her. She had a bathrobe on and slippers. Her hands were flapping like mad at the wrists and she kept mouthing words that Brett couldn't make out. She turned and saw him standing there and her face was panic, worse than his father's. She pointed her finger in the direction of his room and mouthed, "Go."

Brett put up his hands and then ran to his room, leaving the door open behind him, staying in the doorway looking at the floor. He heard his sister shuffling in her room next door. Her blankets fell to the floor and her bed's springs gave a little. Taking a few steps, quietly, he went over to her door and waited for her to open it. When she came out he put one finger in front of his mouth and shook his head side to side.

She shrugged her shoulders and made a quizzical look.

He waved her into his room and they went and sat on the bed with the door closed. They said nothing because they knew it was bad. Brett knew from looking at his face in the mirror that he had much of his father in him. When he looked at his sister, there on his bed, he saw so much of his mother. It seemed like forever that they sat there, and then Brett moved. He put his hand on top of his sister's and said one thing. "I don't know."

The sun started to peak in through the window. "We have to get ready for school now, I think," said Sarah. "You know how Mom is about us being late. I'm going to go downstairs and get breakfast." She was always so sure of what she was supposed to do, never anxious like Brett. Not when they were younger anyway.

Brett held tight to her hand. "No, not yet. Something is

going on. They're really upset. Something happened to Jonathan. Maybe he got arrested." But Brett knew that's not what it was, because then they would just be screaming, not crying.

"We can just ask," said Sarah. "We didn't do anything wrong. They can't yell at us because he did something."

"They can yell at us whenever they want," said Brett.

Sarah took her hand away and crossed her arms. "You're always afraid of everything."

"I'm not afraid of everything. There are things that I should be afraid of."

The door to his bedroom opened and there stood their mother, her face red and wet, and hair in front of it. Brett hated the way she looked right then. It stayed in his mind forever, along with another face she made, years later. It brought out the misery, made it plain to him that something was wrong. He wanted to throw himself out of his window and burn alive in the gasses of the sun.

Sarah stood and hugged their mother who then cried on top of her head. Brett watched in awe, wishing he knew how to deal with emotions like his sister did.

Their father came to the top of the stairs with his jacket on, still wearing sweat pants. Unable to look at them, he kept his eyes on the car keys in his hand. "We have to go," he said to their mother.

"Brett," said their mother, "we need to go somewhere. We need you to stay home with your sister. You're both staying home from school today." That was something they would normally jump up and down over, but not now, not this time.

Sarah broke away from her. "Where's Jonathan? What's going on? Tell us."

Their father came and held her arm. "Not now Sarah. We will explain everything to you guys when we get home."

Joseph went to the car while Barbara hugged them both

and told them not to do anything they knew they shouldn't do. They both asked again what was going on, but she told them to be quiet and to stop asking her. She raised her voice and Brett and Sarah both stood in shock because it was a serious voice and yell, all the motherly kindness was drained from it and it seemed like once that phone had rung something went wrong in her head that changed her forever.

Brett and Sarah ate breakfast cereal. They had the sugary kind their dad always told them to take it easy on and they poured themselves big bowls. Brett knew he was too old to act like this, but with the uneasiness eating at him, it felt like acting younger than his age was the right thing to do. When they finished they went downstairs and turned on the TV, where they watched cartoons.

There was a commercial on. Sarah was sitting on the floor and Brett was on the couch. She turned and looked at him. "Why are you always sad? I'm sad right now, but you're always sad. Why?"

Brett frowned at her. "I'm not always sad."

The show came back on. It was something about a family of bears that lived in a tree. Sarah looked at it and sung some of the words to the theme song and then looked back at him. "Yes you are," she said, "when you're not exercising or swimming in the ocean or something like that."

Brett thought and then he said the same thing he said to her earlier that morning, "I don't know."

Sarah came and sat next to him on the couch and put her head on his shoulder. He rocked back and forth with his arm around her and shook her like Jonathan would have. "You're a good butthead," he said.

When their parents came home it was their mother who came through the door first, her face looking worse than it did before. Brett looked out of the front window and saw their father still sitting in the car with his face against the steering wheel. Before she closed the door behind her she fell to the floor and wept. Brett and Sarah huddled around her. "Jonathan is dead," she said.

Neither of them could speak. All their questions froze. They looked at each other as their faces contorted in pain. They rocked all together. When their father came in he got on the ground and held them too. Then Sarah sat in his lap and they cried on one another.

After a while like that Sarah asked what had happened. Jonathan was out drinking with his friends, Bobby Reed, Joe Seakus, and Norman Acardi. It was Norman's father, a police officer, who called and told them Jonathan was dead. They were on the roof of an abandoned strip mall that was three stories tall. Jonathan was drunk and fell off the side. He died immediately, Norman's father said.

CHAPTER 12

25 years later Brett and Sarah are at the same spot in their childhood home, standing awkwardly for a second before they realize they should hug. Sarah is all in with her arms wrapped around Brett and her head on his chest. Brett keeps one hand on his side and pats her back with the other while looking around, assessing his surroundings. The house hasn't changed much, it's just dustier.

"How you holding up?" he says, while stepping back. He looks at the kitchen table where the mail is piled. There's a bloodstain on it, dried and blotchy. He assumes that's where their mother hit her head.

Sarah shrugs and frowns. "I'm alright, I guess. As good as can be expected. You?"

Brett walks to the kitchen sink and gets a sponge, runs it under the sink and squeezes it out. "Yeah, I'm okay. Feel lousy, but like you said, it's to be expected." Water runs on the table and drips on to the floor from the sponge as he wipes off the blood. Red gets on his hand and he washes it in the sink after throwing out the sponge.

There's a screeching sound as Sarah pulls out a chair and sits down. "I got here yesterday but was dealing with so much to bother cleaning up."

A dead potted plant is on the windowsill above the sink. Brett picks it up and looks at it.

"We'll have time to start cleaning later," Sarah says, "Sit down, and relax."

Brett drops the thing in the trash. "No reason to keep a dead plant." He catches eyes from Sarah that tell him, better than words could, that he needs to slow down. Sitting next to her, he says, "What was she like when you saw her yesterday?"

Elbows on the table and head rested in hands, she says, "She was already gone. She was just a light pulse by the time I got there. It was awful really. It's probably better that she didn't hang on too long. I can't imagine what things would have been like for her."

A panorama of misery plays itself out in Brett's mind. His mother in a nursing home somewhere in Madison Park, her body riddled with bedsores. "God."

She lightly touches his hand. Despite having the same fair complexion, there's a striking difference between the softness of hers and the roughness of his. His fingers are cut and bent slightly at the joints. The palms are calloused. Her hands don't show any wounds. "You don't have to be here long, okay. Help me get things straightened up. We'll throw most of this stuff out. Then you can go and I'll deal with selling the place. I've already called a realtor."

Biting the inside of his mouth, Brett says, "That's not right. I want to help."

There's a clock hanging on the far wall that's still ticking and Sarah turns her head to look at it. "No, you don't. And that's okay, really. I can take care of this and then neither of us will have to be back here again."

He scoffs at that. "This fucking place. The town, I mean. Just driving around it brings everything back. I mean, some of the businesses have changed. Like that deli we used to go to, I drove past and saw it's a 7-11 now. But that's just surface stuff. Everything's the same. Maybe a little shittier, like everything else."

"Always the cheery one."

"Like you disagree?"

"I don't actually, I just don't dwell on it. Yeah, things bother me, but I don't want this place to define me. Maybe it has already, but I'm doing my best so I just swallow it and keep pushing. If I let it drag me down I'm afraid I'll never be able to pull myself up."

Reaching across the table to grab the mail, Brett half smiles, "I hear ya, I just don't want to run in to people, I guess."

Sarah pauses for a second and looks at him, opens her mouth like she's going to say something but it's like her tongue is frozen.

"What?" says Brett.

Sarah spits it out fast. Her face is like she bit into a lemon. "I saw Bobby Reed yesterday. At the 7-11. I had to get out of the hospital. I don't know why. The places are awful. They smell bad. He followed me out to the car and called me a whore." She laughs at the memory, nervously, trying to soothe it. "Then I get the call from the hospital that Mom is dead. It's like, hey, welcome back, asshole."

Brett scrunches his face. "Wait, what?"

"Oh forget it. He's a loser."

"You're fucking right he is. Too bad he's not dead already. Did he say anything else to you?"

"No, okay, no. Jesus, Brett, I shouldn't have even told you. Can you leave it, please?"

He huffs and turns forward. "I just, fuck, you know. Never, they can never leave us alone."

"We won't see them again."

Brett puts his hand down on the table harder than he realizes and it makes his sister jump. "You can't be so sure about that. You know how those guys are. They all talk to each other, they know everybody. Fucking townies, I swear. This place is the biggest small town on fucking earth."

"We can clean this stuff up and then you can get out of here and never come back. Just calm down. Don't be such a dick, could you? Like, when was the last time I saw you? And you have to act like this right out of the gate. You know, Brett, you talk about how this place hasn't changed. You've been here for what, an hour? You're the one that hasn't changed."

It hits him like a fence pole through the chest because it's true. All he can do is sigh.

Sarah turns to him with softer eyes, the anger drained from her. "I'm sorry, okay. I shouldn't have said that."

"What can I say, you got me."

"Hey, maybe we can do something fun while we're here. You know, remember how we used to go to the beach when we were kids before Jonathan died. We frickin' loved it. I was thinking that maybe we could do that, just you and me. Maybe bring back some good memories."

Brett pretend-smiles. "That'd be awesome."

A day later, they go down the shore in Sarah's Volkswagen. As she drives, he watches her. There's that junk food habit she's still got, he knows that, but you wouldn't know it from looking at her. No over thirty gut on her yet. He figures it must be from the nerves because her fidgeting is endless.

She's aged, but not much. Her jaw line and lips are the same as their mother's were. If she ever has kids those traits could be passed down. She won't though, he thinks. Not with what happened to her. Who, he thinks, would want to bring a kid into the world after the childhood they had.

At the beach, Brett's the first to go in the water. It feels like ice on his feet, but the sand is comforting in between his toes. When he walks in to his waist he closes his eyes and thinks about being a kid, about throwing a waterlogged foam football with his brother and then getting out and eating sandwiches his mother made that he accidentally got sand in. Coming up from behind him, Sarah puts her freezing hands on his shoulders before disappearing under the water. Sometimes in the Atlantic you can see down to the bottom, but not today. The water is a dark mixture of green and blue. She pops up a few yards away and waves before she goes under again.

From the water he can see families walking along the beach. There are kids building sand castles, one boy crying because his keeps crumbling and he stands and kicks it and his father asks him what's the matter with him. Brett remembers building a sand castle with Sarah. Jonathan came and kicked it and then they all threw sand at each other.

When they went to the beach as a family, all five of them, his father would pick them up and toss them in the water. They kept track of how far he could throw them. Even strangers would look and laugh. It stopped when they got too big. A year after Jonathan died they tried to go to the beach. They were halfway down, somewhere on the parkway, and the parents started fighting. Brett can't remember what it was over, like he can't remember what most of what their fights were over. Maybe directions. Maybe traffic. Maybe a noise the car was making. Probably money had something to do with it. Sarah cried when they turned around and drove home. Brett didn't look at anyone for the rest of the day. He went to his room when they got home and threw a tennis ball against the wall.

"How is work?" says Sarah to him, when they both get out and sit back on a blanket. They both have sand all over. Sarah's hair is wet and it looks black. They're each turning red. Sarah puts on sunscreen. Brett doesn't.

When Brett was younger he would cringe when people asked him what he wanted to be when he grew up. He had no idea and it made him feel behind everyone else, deficient. "It's work," he says. Nobody hassles me and it pays the bills, sorta."

She smiles. "Tell me about it."

"How about you? Still at the same place?"

"Yeah, the thrift store. I like it. I feel responsible for it. I like talking to the customers. I can take off when I want, pretty much. Like now. I've been there so long at this point that they really let me do what I want. It's a good deal, really it is, but I think I'm capable of more."

"I know you are."

She smiles again at him.

On the drive back, Brett's in the passenger seat again. "I can stay, you know. I don't want you to be here by yourself."

She looks at him. "You don't have to protect me."

"I want to."

She breathes heavily. "I don't think it's good for either of us, really. Don't worry about it. I can handle this."

When they pull into the driveway of the house Brett can tell right away that something is wrong. He narrows his eyes. Glass is shattered in their front picture window. There's a gaping hole. He throws open the door and runs across the lawn before Sarah puts the car in park. He runs to the door and realizes she has the keys so he runs back for them.

Inside, there's a brick on the carpet by the window. It has a piece of paper stuck to it to by a rubber band. Brett's hands are shaking as he picks it up. He breaks the rubber band and takes the paper, lets the brick fall to the ground with a thud. Sarah comes in the door and looks at him.

Brett unfolds the paper. Handwriting, sloppy, in black pen, says, "Get out of here, slut." He throws it to the ground.

Sarah walks towards him. "What is it, Brett? What does it say?" She goes to the paper that he threw on the ground, but he steps on it.

"I am staying here with you until this is done."

CHAPTER 13

Dan sits in the parking lot ten minutes before his shift starts and picks up his cell phone. The first time he calls it goes to a message that says voicemail for the number hasn't been set up. He hangs up and calls again. This time there's a groggy voice on the other end.

"Mom said yesterday that you were going to visit her at the nursing home today." He pauses and listens to the reply. "I don't want you to let her down. She's looking forward to it, alright? So make sure you go, no matter what. I'll find out if you don't." He sighs and then listens again. "Yes, yes you do. You do need a baby sitter, Shane."

When he walks into the lobby of the Madison Park Police Department, Norman Acardi is there, surrounded by a circle of officers. Everyone is laughing and talking at a volume that hurts Dan's ears. They don't notice him. He walks over to a portly secretary with high red hair and three chins and says good morning.

"How are the girls?" she says.

"Making their daddy tired," says Dan. They both laugh and Dan goes in the locker room with the gym bag containing his uniform hanging over his shoulder.

Dan's wife died of cancer three years ago. The year she died was his first year on the force. It should have been a good year. The doctors said it would be fast, but it felt like forever. He cried every time he had to unclog their bathtub drain because of all her hair in it. He and a host of baby sitters are raising his two daughters – ages 7 and 9.

When Dan comes out dressed and ready for his shift, Norman is still in the lobby, talking now to only one person. Patting the other officer on the shoulder, he says, "Listen,

I'll talk to you later, alright pal." The officer keeps talking, but Norman walks away from him anyway.

Dan nods his head. "Good Morning Officer Acardi."

Norman puts his hands on Dan's shoulders. "Danny, how you been?"

"Oh, I'm alright. Busy. Tired. Same old."

"Good. Good. Hey, listen, I heard you were running for the union president thing too."

Dan pauses. He's not sure what to say at first and Norman stares at him. "Yep, I figured I'd give it a shot."

Norman gives half a smile. The grease in his hair is shining. "That's fair, man. That's fair. I just wanted to tell you, I like you, you know. You're a good guy and I plan on keeping things clean, alright."

Dan tries his best to smile fully. "That's great. Me too."

Norman extends a hand. "Well good. Good. Hey listen, I better get on the road and start my shift."

"Me too," says Dan.

Norman leaves the building and gets in his unmarked car. Dan walks towards Waxman, who he sees coming in through another door at the end of his shift.

"Hey Nichols," says Waxman. "I had a slow night, my friend. May you have the same luck."

Dan waves to him on his way out, wondering if it was a good idea to take the guy's advice. In the parking lot, as he walks to his cruiser, he hears Acardi's voice, yelling at someone. "Are you fucking stupid?" Dan can't see him and doesn't hear anyone respond so he assumes Acardi is on the phone. "Did I say I wanted you to do anything, you fucking moron?"

Dan gets to his car and opens the door. When he sits down and closes the door, he can still hear Acardi yelling.

"You better fucking hope her fucking brother isn't around. That's all I've got to say. Then, if he is, we've got a whole 'nother problem on our hands."

Dan has no idea who Acardi was talking to or what he's talking about and hopes it stays that way. When Dan drives out of the lot he passes Acardi, still leaning on his car and on the phone, and the two of them make eye contact. Acardi's face is red and sweaty. Rodney is there too, back by the trunk of the cruiser, standing with his arms crossed glaring hard at Dan.

Dan's got his suspicions about Rodney and Norman, and about the whole rest of the department; the whole town does. He'll hear people talking about the police department when he goes to one of his daughter's softball games. They'll say how they don't trust the cops and they'll be in the middle of telling a story about how some shit officer yelled at them or drove like an asshole or treated their concern about people doing drugs in front of their house like they had a million better things to do and then as soon as they realize he's there they'll stop the conversation dead. Once he heard somebody on line at the Stop and Shop say how they thought the cops were probably the reason for the uptick in crime over the past few years and for all the drugs.

Shane talks to those two. He knows it. He's seen them leaning in to their cars over by the Ford plant when no one realized he was around the corner. Shane's got money, but no job. You don't have to be a rocket scientist to figure out the reason for that.

When he was a kid Dan told everyone he wanted to be a police officer because the cops were the good guys. He wanted to be one of them. He still wants to be one of them, but now it's because it pays the bills and the bills have to be paid.

Picking up the radio, he tells the dispatcher he's in service. Before he can put the radio down he's dispatched to a house he knows well, where an old friend lived.

CHAPTER 14

Sarah is the one to call the police. In a calm but wavering voice she says the house has been vandalized.

Brett rolls his eyes. Pacing back and forth, the veins in his hands and forearms are pronounced.

"Now let's see what good they do."

Sarah wants to tell him to give it a chance, that maybe things have changed, but she doesn't say it because she doesn't believe it. "Don't freak out at them."

Brett stops pacing. He's in the middle of the living room, standing on the broken glass with the brick now clenched in his hands. "We'll see." Then he starts walking back and forth again, looking outside and then looking at the floor.

Sarah pulls over the kitchen garbage can and puts the large pieces of broken glass in it and then sits at the kitchen table. There's a tiny bit of dried blood from where their mother fell still on it that Brett missed when cleaning. She puts her head in her hands and runs her fingers in her hair.

Brett looks at her and stands still. He pauses and his face loses some of its tension. "You okay?" he says. His grip on the brick is so hard it's hurting his fingers. He takes a breath and puts it down on the floor and then walks over to his sister and puts his hand on her shoulder.

There's no answer to his question. She spots the speck of dried blood and runs her fingers over it. Nothing will get that stain out.

There's a knock on the door. A man says, "Madison Park PD." Brett crosses his arms and Sarah goes and turns the knob.

"Danny Nichols," she says when she opens the door, "is

that you?" She hugs him before thinking about it. Dan returns the hug then she pulls herself back. She holds onto a strand of her hair that's fallen in front of her face and looks at him.

Dan steps back and looks at the broken window and the rest of the front of the house. "I knew this address was familiar when I heard it," says Dan, with his head turned sideways. "And look at you," he says, looking back at her, with his hands out as if he's appraising something, "Sarah, all grown up." Pointing at the window, he says, "This what you called about, I take it?"

Sarah puts her hands on her hips. "Of course."

Brett comes up behind Sarah and she can feel him looking over her shoulder. Dan looks up at him. "Well holy shit. Look at this. Jesus did you get big. I mean jacked." He looks up and down at Brett.

Sarah motions for Dan to come inside and he does. He offers a hand to Brett and when Brett extends his own Dan takes it in two hands and shakes it. While still holding Brett's hand, he looks over to Sarah and says, "Hey, listen guys, I heard about your mom from the boys in EMS. I'm sorry, really."

"Thanks," says Brett.

Sarah smiles at him. "Thank you, Danny. Thank you. Do your parents still live in town?"

"Oh no," says Dan. "My Dad passed a few years back and my Mom is in a nursing home over in New Brunswick."

"Oh, I'm sorry," says Sarah.

Dan shrugs. "Hey, it's life. What're you gonna do?"

"Tell me about it," says Sarah.

Brett breaks free from Dan's handshake and walks over to the window. "So let's talk about this."

Dan comes over. "Of course, when did you find it?"

"Few minutes ago," Brett says.

"We were at the beach," says Sarah. "We wanted a day

away from all of this so we went to the beach, before it got too cold. When we came back this is what we found."

Brett has the note in his hand, crumpled up. The brick is nearby. He shows the note to Dan. "And we found this shit. This fucking note, stuck to the brick with a rubber band."

Dan reads it. "Oh, for Christ's sake. This damn town. I'm sorry guys."

"Nothing you need to be sorry for," says Brett. "Just do your job."

Sarah gives him a look that Dan doesn't notice. Brett sees it and then looks at the carpet.

"Of course," says Dan. He takes the note from Brett and pauses, reads it again. "I'm gonna hold on to this, alright? Evidence."

Brett goes to a closet and gets out a vacuum. "Might be small pieces of glass in there," he says.

Before he plugs it in and turns it on, Dan says, "I'll go look at the outside."

Sarah goes with him. She can hear the vacuum buzzing through the broken window. Dan looks at the window and then walks to the road. "Could have been thrown from a vehicle," he says. He looks at Sarah, "You guys holding up alright?"

"I guess. Before this anyway. I mean, I'm okay." Then she gestures over to the house. "I can never tell with this guy. But how about you?"

"I've been on the department a few years now," says Dan. "Worked on the fire department before that. I've got two girls."

Sarah touches his arm. "That's wonderful."

Dan nods. "Yep. It's tough. Just me and them. Lost their mother a while ago to cancer."

"Oh Dan. Dan, I'm so sorry."

"Thank you. It's alright. We're holding together. They're a pleasure to be around."

"I'm sure they are."

"I didn't think I would ever see either of you back here,"

says Dan. "Where do you guys live?"

Sarah's looking in every direction, still nervous. "Oh, I live in Brooklyn. Brett lives in Pennsylvania. Nothing spectacular for either of us."

"Sounds alright though, better than here I bet."

Sarah scoffs. "That's not too hard," she says, with her hand on her chin.

Dan looks at the window again and writes some things down in a small notepad. "Let's go in. I want to talk to you both and tell you how things are gonna go."

When they go in Brett is standing in front of the door, waiting for them. He leans his head down and towards Dan, expecting something.

"Here's what's gonna happen," says Dan. "I'm gonna go door to door and I'm gonna see if anybody saw anything. It could take a while. I'll give you guys a call tomorrow and let you know what I find out. Hopefully we'll get some info, hopefully somebody saw something."

Brett crosses his arms again. "You're gonna do all this yourself?"

Dan's demeanor changes. "Yeah, it's a big town."

"And a big police force," says Brett.

Dan looks at Sarah and then back at Brett. "And we will figure out who did this, alright. Do not worry."

Brett points at nothing in particular and says, "The note. There are a few people I can think of that would write something like that. You know who they are."

"I do," says Dan.

Brett motions with his hands to Sarah like he wants her to say something. She shakes her head no and he rolls his eyes and says it anyway. "You know, Officer Dan, she ran in to Bobby fucking Reed yesterday at the 7-11 and he called her a whore. Would you fucking believe that?"

"As a matter of fact, I would."

"Alright then, so you know where to start."

"I've got this, okay. I know how to do my job. You guys just relax."

Sarah nods at that and Brett continues looking at the floor like nothing was said.

When Dan leaves Sarah punches Brett in the shoulder, not lightly. He rubs it with his hand.

"You're such a fucking dick. Why do have to act like that?"

He steps away from her, still rubbing his arm. "I didn't act like anything. You have to be firm or people walk all over you."

There are tears in Sarah's eyes. "You don't know it was Bobby that did that."

"You're kidding me, right?"

"But c'mon, can't you just leave it. So what? We'll let the police handle it and we move on, like I said from the beginning."

Brett pushes one of the kitchen chairs into the table, hard. "Oh yeah, let the police handle it, like they did when Jonathan died."

"It's fucking Danny you asshole."

"So. I haven't seen him in twenty years. I don't know who he is. He could be like the rest of them. Like everybody else."

The tears flow down Sarah's cheeks. "You act like you have a monopoly on suffering, you know that. Just because you wear what they did to you on your face doesn't mean you're the one that was hurt the worst. You out of everyone have no fucking idea. No fucking clue."

"I'm sorry." He hugs her and she puts her head on his shoulder. Together they lean against the front door. "I'm sorry," he says again.

After a minute she breaks away. "You're still an asshole."

"I know."

CHAPTER 15

Dan sits in his patrol car going over his notes in a large parking lot off of route one. The sun is going down. Hopefully it will be a good peaceful shift and he can relax.

The optics would be bad inside the department if he goes right to Bobby Reed, if the first thing he does is go and question a friend of Norman Acardi. It would only be a vandalism charge, maybe harassment, but he's heard of spats over lesser things. There's the rumor that Acardi beat the piss out of an elderly neighbor with his own walker for calling and telling dispatch he drove erratically. Then there's the one about how Acardi made an officer he had a beef with quit by sitting in front of his house in his car all night long for a week straight sending dick pictures to his wife via text. These are rumors, of course, but Dan's hunch is that there's truth to them. So rather than poke the bear, he's going to start by talking to neighbors, make it look like the last thing he did was take the Bernauers' word for anything.

The first neighbor didn't see or hear anything. Neither did the second. The third person, a single guy with a beer gut who was mad that Dan interrupted his Giants versus Jets game, says that yes, he did heard tires screeching, but didn't get up to look at what was going on.

The fourth neighbor, on the corner in a grey house with Christmas lights on it in September, is a woman Dan and the rest of the force know well. Ms. Johnson used to call about something at least once a week. She knew Dan since he was little and came around for candy on Halloween. For entertainment, she sat in front of her window with the curtain pulled back and watched the neighborhood. Over time she'd been told by some in town to mind her own fucking business. So the calls only came now when they concerned her or her home, but they still came.

She called him Officer Danny when she answered the door, made him tea in a chipped cup with flowers on it. Yes, she had heard something, she told him. While cleaning out the litter box, she heard tires screeching and went over to look out the window. She didn't see anything happen, but she saw an old white van. It was going like a bat out of hell. Dan says thank you and finishes the tea.

When she opens the door to let him out he turns and asks her why she didn't called it in. She tells him that she learned a long time ago that most people didn't want to hear from old ladies like her.

Dan sits and thinks about that and hopes to God he doesn't feel that way when he's older, but knows he probably will.

There's one more neighbor that saw the white van. She too couldn't say much about it. Didn't get any plates. Didn't see the person driving it. She's a stay at home mom with two kids under three. She heard the tires as she was taking them out of her car, back from a doctor's visit, and turned and saw it pulling around the corner, by Ms. Johnson's house.

He's reading his notes from that visit when Acardi pulls up in his unmarked car next to him and rolls down the window.

"You go to that vandalism call, officer?" he says. He is looking into Dan's cruiser, down at his note pad.

Dan sees where his eyes are focused and he closes the pad and puts it down on the passenger seat. "I did. Smashed window. Nothing too bad."

Acardi nods and looks over at the pad again. "That's good. Hey I hope we get another slow night tonight, right?"

"Oh yeah," says Dan. "You and me both."

Acardi has his hand outside of his vehicle and he's

drumming on the door with his fingers, two of his rings are clicking on the metal. He has sunglasses perched on top of his head. "I bet those girls keep you busy."

"They sure do," says Dan. "But it's good I can be with them."

Acardi doesn't say anything for a minute or two and ignores the fact that Dan is looking at him, wondering what he came over to him for. "Listen, why don't you not worry about that vandalism, alright?"

Dan looks at him cockeyed, but not surprised. "It's no problem."

"Oh, I know," says Acardi, "but listen, you relax. You deserve it, I know. Maybe call that brother of yours, make sure he's staying out of trouble. I'll take care of the vandalism."

"You know where it happened? Whose house it was?"

Acardi slaps the car door with his hand, the rings make a loud clack, but he pretends he didn't do it out of frustration. He smiles. His teeth are white and perfect. The pock marks on his face scrunch up. He itches his scalp with a finger, carefully so not to mess up his gelled hair. "I know, Dan. I know. All that stuff is the past, alright."

Dan doesn't commit to what Acardi wants. He nods enough so the guy will leave. When he finally does, Dan looks out at the passing traffic and thinks about the long shadow that the past casts over the present. He thinks about what he heard Acardi saying earlier on the phone and wishes he had had headphones in or something.

CHAPTER 16

The funeral's on a rainy Sunday with grey clouds that hang over Brett and Sarah as they leave the house, avoiding puddles scattered around the lawn. Brett drives them in his truck because Sarah's too upset to drive. He throws out old coffee cups and newspapers sitting on the passenger seat before she gets in. On the drive over they're accompanied only by the sound of the rain and the wiper blades.

Brett thinks about the other funerals he's been too. Those of his family. There isn't too much that's different. They've always used the same cemetery, the same church. The weather's always been gloomy. The only difference is that with each new death fewer and fewer people show up to mourn.

The first part of the service is outside the church. And though everyone's gathered around with umbrellas the rain's stopped. There's a stone marker with their mother's name on it. It's in between their father's and Jonathan's headstones. They were black once, but they're grey now.

An elderly aunt comes over and puts her arm around Sarah, who leans in against her. No one comes near Brett. There's a rumbling sound of a car nearby that's distracting him from the Bible passage some church lady with polyester pants is reading. Across the cemetery green is a beige Oldsmobile with rust above the tires.

The church lady starts on about walking through the valley of the shadow of death and not fearing evil and Brett shakes his head, focuses his eyes instead on the car. There are two lanky people with thin brown mustaches and T-shirts with the sleeves cut off smoking cigarettes and hanging their arms out the car windows. They're turned in Brett's direction with faces he's seen before. But not in a long time.

Rage turns up Brett's heart rate and he takes steps forward before Sarah grabs him by the wrist. With startling resemblance to her mother, she mouths, "What?" He points towards the car and opens his eyes wide with a tight jaw. People are looking at them now. The church lady pauses her Bible reading for a beat and then continues. A sad look from Sarah gets Brett to back pedal and join the family, but he watches the car the entire time until the service moves inside.

In the church, a pastor that didn't know their mother says a few things about her. Nobody cares. They're not listening. He once calls her by the wrong name and no one lifts their head.

Afterward, there's socializing in the social hall. Some old ladies made some soggy sandwiches. Sarah cries and talks to everyone. She bites her nails and her makeup spreads on her face.

Standing over Sarah as she drinks coffee, Brett, with the veins on his neck protruding, says, "You see those two goons outside earlier?" The church lady with the polyester pants is at the table with Sarah. Her eyes are on Brett and are the size of silver dollars.

Sarah's expression is worn out. "Yeah, I saw them. What do you want me to do? Leave it, alright."

Shaking his head, he says "I'm not leaving shit."

Their mother was cremated and now all they have of her is some ashes in a metal container, like the rest of their family. Sarah'll keep it. She's better at memories and that sort of thing.

That night they drink a bottle of whisky and don't say a word to one another. Sarah passes out on the couch and Brett sleeps next to her on the floor. The sound of her breathing in and out calms him, like ocean waves. They keep his mind off of other things. He tries not to snore, but does anyway and she wakes him up in the middle of the night by hitting him in the head with a pillow.

In the morning, Brett calls Fred to tell him that he'll be a few more days off of work, says he's gonna stick around until his sister's got the place ready to sell. Fred tells him it's cool, to take as much time as he needs. He says things are working out better with Jay after he gave him a talking to about smoking pot before work. In a few days he'll take him hunting and show him his way around a gun, like he's done with Brett many times.

Two days later, against Sarah's wishes, Brett goes to the police department in the late afternoon to talk to Dan. The receptionist with the big red hair says he isn't in the station, he's out on the road, but she gives Brett a number he can reach him on. He says thank you to the woman and walks through the lobby with his head down, conscious of his scar.

On the way to his truck in the parking lot, he stops cold. There's a figure. Brett's overcome by the urge to vomit. He can't move. The person is getting into a black car, like a cop car, but unmarked. The face is unmistakable.

Norman Acardi looks up once he's in the car and they both stare at each other, speechless. Acardi turns on the engine and drives away. Brett still can't move. He watches the car pull away and wishes the world were ending. There's pain in his hands and he looks down at them, realizing he's dug his fingernails into his palms.

When he's able to walk back to his truck he gets in and punches the steering wheel. He forgets what he went to the station for in the first place. It's hard for him to breath. He sees Sarah's face, crying. It's a younger face. He sees his father screaming. His mother crying. Then he sees all the blood in his parent's bedroom. The memories are from different times, different situations, but they congeal and hit him like a ton of bricks.

A half an hour passes by of him sitting in his truck with his eyes closed, trying to control his breathing. He takes his phone out of his pocket and is about to call the number the redheaded receptionist gave him when Dan pulls up next to him in his cruiser and they both get out.

"I want to know what you've found out," says Brett.

"What's going on, Brett? Calm down."

"No," he says. "Maybe I'll calm down when you tell me what you're going to do about these people harassing my sister, after all the shit she went through here."

"I don," begins Dan, but he's cut off.

"And you didn't have the balls to tell me Norman Acardi was a cop here. How the fuck did that happen?"

"Of course he's a cop, Brett. His father was a cop. You know how it is. Plus, what else is the guy gonna do?" He doesn't wait for an answer. "Look, I learned from a neighbor that a white van was seen driving away, fast. That might have been it, but I've got nothing else to go on other than that."

There's another officer walking through the parking lot. The guy's arms are covered with tattoos. Brett notices Dan and the officer look at each other. There's definite tension there. The guy runs his eyes up and down Brett, and he can feel it, but he knows if he says something or addresses it in anyway he'll fly off the handle.

"Nothing else to go on?" he says, turning his head fully from the guy and back to Dan. "God, it's like you're trying to let this go. I'll tell you what you do, you look at Acardi and his friends and you see who's got the white van, and there you go. Start with Bobby Reed for fucks sake. I think you've got reason enough, don't you?"

"I do and I will, but we can't go making assumptions."

"Of course we can. And shit, that reminds me of one more thing. You know Joe and Kenny fucking Seakus came to my mother's funeral today. You gonna do anything about that?"

"What'd they do?"

"They sat in their damn ghetto roller."

"There's not much I can do about that, man. Sitting in a car isn't really harassment."

"Of course it fucking is. Jesus Christ, why the hell else would they be there but to harass us? Grow a pair of balls and do your job, Dan."

"Just because I'm not doing what you want me to do doesn't mean I'm not doing it. You don't know the first thing about police work."

Brett balls up one fist and puts the other hand on Dan's shoulder, grabbing his uniform. "Either you deal with them or I will."

Dan moves aside Brett's hand with his forearm. "You put your hand on me again and I'll knock you out and arrest you for assaulting an officer, got it? Now look, maybe the best thing for you to do is just ignore them, okay. These aren't really people you want to get involved with again."

Brett backs away and starts towards his truck. "Jesus, you're just like the rest of them."

CHAPTER 17

1995

In the years following Jonathan's death, things only went downhill for the Bernauer family. Joseph was fired from his job as client manager at the advertising company. He couldn't stay organized. Missed meetings. Bungled assignments. The final straw was when he told a client he didn't give a fuck when their deadlines were. That was the first year.

The next year he got another similar position. They fired him within the first six months. He would cry in his cubical and they told him it wasn't working out. Nothing more than that. It just wasn't working out.

For six months he looked for other jobs in advertising while collecting unemployment. He put on forty pounds and added a chin. People talked about the booming economy. He said, "What booming economy?" Every flat surface in the house had an overdue bill notice on it, big bold letters in all caps that Brett learned to associate with screaming matches and slamming doors.

Eventually, Joseph sucked it up and gave up on advertising, got a job as a dispatcher for a moving company. He sat at a desk surrounded by phones and had people yelling at him for twelve hours a day in a room that smelled like electrical fire and dust. He never saw the sun anymore.

The pain of Jonathan's death never left, they only learned to not pay as much attention to it. The parents, their marriage suffered. People mourn in different ways, they say. Joseph, he wanted to provide, swore nothing would ever happen to either of his other kids. Barbara mourned openly, wanted to talk about Jonathan, barely left the house, stayed in her pajamas, and looked at pictures all the time. She had knots in her hair. They argued about moving on. Neither of them ever did.

Brett went into himself and never fully left. Dan remained his only friend, but the distance there grew. He didn't go off the rails academically, not like Sarah did, but he didn't excel either. After school, he went to his room and did push-ups. When his parents called him down for dinner he told them he wasn't hungry, he wanted to stay in his room. They had to bang on is door and scream until he came out. Then, at the table, with Brett forking something microwaved into his mouth, Joseph would say something like, "Why do you have to make everything so difficult for me?"

Sarah was hanging out with the wrong crowd, as Joseph would say, the same wrong crowd that Jonathan was with when he fell of the roof. Joseph told her he didn't trust those kids, said that he never completely understood what happened to Jonathan. He pushed the police for more information. They said it was an accident. The boys were drinking. Joseph wanted more details. He tried to ask Norman Acardi himself, but Norman's father, the cop, told him on the phone not to harass his son, said he would press charges. Joseph said he didn't give a fuck. They could hall him away in cuffs for all he cared. Barbara threw a dish on the floor and it shattered into a thousand tiny pieces.

Sarah, though she would never admit as much to her parents, told Brett that she hung out with Jonathan's old friends, Norman, Bobby, and Joe, because they reminded her of Jonathan. It was a way to keep him alive. To her parents, she just said she did what she wanted to do. It was her life. "You're not such great parents anyway," Brett heard her say once while he was doing squats in his room, "so why should I listen to you?"

She was in the ninth grade and hanging out in the town's many abandoned buildings with guys in their early twenties. Norman was at the county college, taking up criminal justice. "He knows plenty about being a criminal, that's for sure," is what Joseph would tell Sarah when she would use his studies as an example of why he wasn't such a bad guy.

But he was a bad guy, as far as Brett was concerned, always. Closer in age to Norman and the others, Brett knew more about him than Sarah did. He saw more. They'd gone to the same school when they were younger, before Norman graduated. Brett saw the fights at school that he never got in trouble for. He knew he threatened to punch a teacher for telling him to sit down. There were rumors about the way he was with girls. Plus, Brett didn't like his smug, self-satisfied, acne-covered face. He was an ugly dude that thought he was anything but, both inside and out.

The others weren't any better. Bobby Reed was a sad young man whose parents disappeared when he was a toddler and left him to be cared for by his overweight grandmother who had to go everywhere with a walker that had tennis balls at the bottom of each leg. Joseph and Barbara felt bad for him, but were nevertheless weary of him, even before Jonathan's death.

At 21 he was a full-blown alcoholic and had been for some time before he was even of the legal age. He had a number of DUIs and was one stop away from having his license revoked. He'd been arrested for trying to steal gasoline after he drove away without paying and still had the pump attached to his gas tank.

Joe Seakus lived with his brother Kenny and their father in a trailer that sat up on cinder blocks in the woods somewhere on the southern side of town. The father served a long time in prison for beating a man to death with a pool cue over a spilled beer. When he got out, the mother of his two boys said she had enough of their sorry asses, threw the keys to the trailer at him, and was never seen again.

Joe was almost as bad as Norman as far as the violence went. The only difference was that Joe'd been punished for his sins. He never finished high school. He'd been expelled for a fight and went to juvie. He'd beaten a kid unconscious with a lunch tray.

Norman, though not as hard-looking as Joe and not as down-and-out reckless as Bobby, was in charge of their little trifecta and was the one whom cognizant people in town were most afraid of.

~ ~ ~

It was a Friday in early May, the day when they did it to Sarah. It had been a brutal winter that year. The snow got so high people in Madison Park could barely open their front doors. Telephone wires tore and fell to the ground under the weight of all the ice that had accumulated on them. When the winter ended everyone wanted to be outside as long as they could.

Sarah was walking home from the high school in a tank top. She was alone when Norman pulled up alongside of her. Joe and Bobby were in the backseat. He put his hand on the front passenger seat and told her to get in.

She stayed home from school the next day, told her parents something was wrong with her stomach. They believed her when she came into the kitchen and vomited while they were eating breakfast. They asked her why she was having trouble walking. She told them she wasn't.

When Brett came home from school he opened the door to her bedroom and looked inside at her. She was curled into a ball, asleep. She was holding a stuffed Winnie the Pooh he hadn't seen in years.

She stayed home from school the next day too. The vomiting stopped, but she only left her room to pee and still hadn't eaten anything. Joseph came in to see her when his dispatching shift was over. He sat on her bed as she slept, ran his hand through her light brown hair. Looked at her. Called her his little girl.

They made her go to school the next day. They said as far as they could tell she wasn't sick. Maybe upset about something. Barbara said maybe she was nervous about something in school, a test or something like that. At the end of the day there was a teacher's voice on the answering machine at home. She was asking if everything was alright with Sarah, said she wasn't acting right, wanted to know if something had happened that the school should know about.

She stopped wearing her normal clothes. Sweat pants and baggy shirts were all any one saw her in for two weeks. She stopped putting on her makeup. She stopped combing her hair. She went from eating nothing to eating everything. Her weight gain over days was visible. She went from being out all the time to staying in and watching TV non-stop.

Something happened. Somebody at school told her she was a freak. She cried and ran out of the class. The teacher told her to go to the school crisis counselor.

Then her parents got another call. Barbara went to the school. Sarah sat in the lobby with her knees pulled to her chest and her head down. The crisis counselor was an obese woman with a cheap haircut and flat shoes. She told Barbara that Sarah had all the signs of a traumatic incident, a sexual assault. She asked if anything had happened at home. Barbara said "No, of course not." They brought Sarah into the room and she sat on a chair next to Barbara. She put her arms around her daughter and said, "What happened, baby?"

The counselor put her hands on her knees and bent forward. "This is a safe place, Sarah. You can tell us."

Sarah sobbed. She put her head to her mother's shoulder and her chest heaved. Barbara rocked her back and forth and looked at the counselor for some sign of what she should do. The counselor gave her a box of tissues.

Barbara looked at Sarah. "Did somebody hurt you, baby?" Sarah lifted her head from her mother's shoulder and nodded up and down. Then she told them what happened and Barbara drove her to the police station.

A woman detective took notes while Sarah told her what happened. She said it was three weeks ago. Barbara heard the detective exhale. While writing something down, the detective asked if Sarah still had the underwear she was wearing or if she washed it. Sarah said no; she threw it away.

"Why did you do that, honey?" asked Barbara.

There was a snot bubble on Sarah's nose. "I didn't want you to know."

Barbara pulled her close. "Oh, honey. Honey." The detective brought Sarah into a waiting room and talked to Barbara out in the hallway alone.

"I'm sorry, Mrs. Bernauer," she said, "but with the time that has passed and no clothing to test for semen, it's unlikely we will be able to make an arrest."

"You have to try," Barbara said.

The detective put her hand on Barbara's shoulder. "We will ma'am. We will bring the boys in for questioning."

Barbara looked at the detective with her blood-shot eyes. "They are not boys, do not give me that. They are not fucking boys."

Barbara brought Sarah home and put her in her bed. She gave her chicken noodle soup and said she was sorry and that they loved her.

When she told Joseph he punched a hole in the wall. Brett heard it and came out of his room. His father ran out the door. Tires screeched outside.

That first time that Joseph tracked down Norman Acardi and told him he would kill him, find him while he was sleeping and cut his fucking throat for what he did, the police let him off on a warning on account of the obvious stress he was under. Norman's father said there was no need to press charges at the time.

The second time though, when he punched him and knocked out a tooth, the police arrested him. He sat in the holding cell at the police station for a day. Norman's father came over and told him that if he was ever seen near his son again they would put him in prison for a long time.

Brett knew something had happened, but another two weeks went by and no one had told him what. His sister stayed home from school the entire time on an excused extended absence. Their parents were taking her out and sending her to an all-girls private school, though they could hardly afford it. One day, as Brett sat in the back of the school bus, Dan tapped on his shoulder and pointed out the window. There was an abandoned grocery store with red graffiti on it that said, "Sarah Bernauer is a lying whore."

CHAPTER 18

Brett pulls out of the parking lot of the Madison Park Police Department. The memories are heavy. He can see the way his sister looked. The stress of that time is still on her face. He drives around, fuming and thinking. The whole world is a farce. Justice is made up. There's no such thing as karma. What goes around does not come around.

After pulling into the 7-11 parking lot, he sits with his head in his hands talking to himself. Those old friends of Jonathan's, the ones he was with when he died, the ones that raped Sarah – he remembers where they lived. A plan develops and he pulls out of the lot, searching.

The house Norman Acardi lived in looks much nicer now than it did all those years ago. It was nice then too, but now there's a fountain in the front yard and a man comes out and looks at Brett. He's wearing a tank top and hair is shooting around it from his back and shoulders. He has one eyebrow across his forehead. Acardi doesn't live there and there isn't a white van there anyway, so he drives on.

Memories resurface as he drives down streets he once rode his bike on. There's a memory of him and his brother and his sister all riding their bikes in their flip-flops after coming home from the beach.

A mile down the road, he pulls over next to a lot filled with high grass. There's a boarded up house in the middle of it with a cat on the porch that looks like Al the way it's scowling. If only yellow pages were still a thing he could look up Acardi and figure out the rest from there. He looks at his phone. Nate's always telling him he should be on Facebook. It's a good way to do research on people as long as they don't have high security settings.

He downloads the app, waits for it to open and as soon as his phone screen shows the blue Facebook icon he types in a search for Norman Acardi. The profile picture is stomach churning. Acardi is in his uniform. Officer friendly. There's little info written about him. Only where he works, not where he lives.

The account's got loads of photos, typical for the arrogant prick. Acardi's with a woman, his wife. There are wedding photos. At first Brett scans quickly, more interested in figuring out where the house is, but then he realizes who the woman is. It's Jennifer Kyle. She used to smile at him when they were younger, never talked too much to him, but still gave him the feeling that he was normal, that he could be desirable like the others, that he wasn't some sort of emotional misfit. Of course it was a lie. But maybe she was decent at some point. Some people are born shit, he thinks, some people turn into it.

They've got a house. There's a picture of Norman holding up a realtor sign that says sold. It has a swimming pool and they seem to always have people over to swim in it and barbeque next to it on a grill that's probably worth more than Brett's truck. The neighbor's houses are all just as nice. There are no cars parked on lawns. Brett doesn't know where it is, but there's no indication that Acardi has a white van. He's posted pictures of his two cars, one an SUV and the other a Mustang, and the unmarked police cruiser.

Brett compares Acardi's home to where he lives. Maybe he should be jealous, maybe, but still, he'd rather live in the woods with his cat than surrounded by people obsessed with their cars and their lawns.

He gives up on Acardi, for the time being. Not far from where he is now, he remembers there being a trailer park, not a trailer park with paved roads and trailers that people put porches on and attach American flags to, but a place where the dilapidated trailers sit on cinder blocks, where the broken pavement is littered with beer bottles. Joe and his brother Kenny lived there.

Brett drives to the park. It's 11AM and there's a guy sitting on the pavement with a bottle of Wild Turkey. He watches with blood-shot eyes as Brett passes him. There's a dog walking around without a leash or an owner nearby, some sort of lab mix. The dog looks just as dazed as the drunk.

From memory, he knows the Seakus family lived towards the back. Things look more desperate the further he drives into the place. He's going slow. The trailers at the back look post-apocalyptic. Some are boarded up. They're all sagging, ready to crumble. Aluminum siding is hanging off.

When he sees it, he remembers it. He went there with Jonathan once, against their parents' wishes. Against his own wishes. Jonathan had teased him about being scared until he gave in and tagged along. Once the place was white. Now it's yellow, the color of old newspaper. There's a window in the front with a fist-sized hole like somebody threw a rock through it. There's a green metal awning over the entrance that's got rust on it. On the side opposite Brett, there's a metal bumper of an old car sticking out. Letting off the break, he inches closer. The car's a beige Oldsmobile, *the* Oldsmobile.

"Motherfucker." After putting the truck in park in the middle of the road, he makes quick work of the taillights with his hammer. The shattering sound of the glass doesn't bother him. Let them come out.

Brett k-turns. There's a guy walking around. He's heavy, wearing a tracksuit. Despite his weight, his face is gaunt. Heroin. He's seen people stuck on it out in the decaying cities of northeastern PA, but it's hit Jersey harder. They make eye contact. He's about to slam on the gas when the guy speaks.

"Brett?"

He keeps rolling.

The fat man talks again. "Brett Bernauer."

He stops, looks at the guy in the rear view. He's coming closer, sort of waddling. Brett looks at his hammer sitting on the passenger seat and rolls down the window. The guy puts his hands on the door, there's filth under the fingernails.

The guy extends a hand for Brett to shake. "It's me, yo."

Brett squints at him. He shakes his hand, doesn't say anything.

"Shane, Danny's brother. Shit, don't go acting like you don't remember me."

Brett takes a longer look at him. "Well, hell," he says, "I hardly recognized you."

Shane looks down, shakes his head subtly. "I know, man. I know. The years ain't been easy on me. But hey, what're you doing back in town?"

"My mom passed. Had to deal with all that stuff, you know."

"Shit man. I'm sorry man. That's rough."

Brett nods.

"What're you doing in the park? You stopping by to see Joe and Kenny?"

There's an uncomfortable pause. "Just driving around some of the old hangouts. Seeing what's changed, what hasn't."

"I hear you, man, but shit, not much has changed, I'll tell you that."

Brett half smiles at the truth of it. "I can tell."

"My brother know you're back? I'm sure he'd like to see you."

"Yep, he knows. Saw him a few days ago."

"That's cool. That's cool." He slaps his hand on the truck door and looks around him on the street. "Listen, I best be going, but it was good to see you, bro."

"You too."

They shake again and Brett drives off. He shakes his head at the way Shane looks and thinks about what his life must be like now. Some people are born shit and some people turn into it.

One more place left to check. Like Joe and Kenny's, Bobby's old place is falling apart. And there's a car on the lawn. There's cars all over the place, few of them appear to be in working condition. There's a Honda Civic on the street in front of the old house and the driveway's filled with similar-looking cars. Brett looks. No van. He starts to pull away. There's a wooden fence in the back of the driveway. Peaking over it is the top of a white van. Brett slams on his breaks and gets a better look. It's all the evidence necessary.

He drives out of the neighborhood and goes back to the 7-11, pulls out his phone. Nate answers.

"You in the mood to come out to Jersey?"

CHAPTER 19

Norman Acardi is laying in his bed next to his wife, Jennifer, playing Candy Crush on his phone. She's reading some book with midwife in the title. She's told him what it was about, but he wasn't listening. She's got a towel around her head, her hair still wet from the shower. She's got long pink fingernails, spray-tanned skin.

She worked for years as a receptionist at a doctor's office, hated it. With the money Norman brings home, there's really no need for her to work. He told her to quit, stay around and make the house look nice.

They've known each other their entire lives. Jennifer is younger, grew up being a little frightened of Norman. The fear of him made him attractive to her too. Her father was a cop and encouraged the relationship with Norman, said that marriage to a cop was a good thing, stable, always money coming in, food on the table. Jennifer's mother had reservations. She wanted Jennifer to go off to college and find somebody educated. Nobody listened to her.

Jennifer puts the book down on her lap, puts a hand on his thigh. She can feel his muscles. "When we gonna talk about starting a family baby? We only got so much time you know. I mean, I only got so much time. You guys can make babies till the day you die."

He taps on his phone, doesn't say anything, or look at her. He's in an undershirt and boxer shorts. His gold chain is around his neck.

"Huh, baby?" she says.

He rolls his eyes. "I don't wanna talk about this now, Jen. I had a long day. I'm tired, alright? Why do we always have to talk about shit?"

"Sorry honey. It's important is all." She picks back up the book.

Norman's phone starts to ring, caller ID says it's Shane. "I gotta take this," Norman says, and he gets up and leaves the room. He makes sure he closes the door behind him, walks down the hall, puts the phone to his ear. "Better be important."

Shane tells him who he ran in to.

"I know. I saw him too. Fucker was at the police station. I don't know what he was doing. Son of bitch thinks somebody around here is gonna listen to him? And to his crazy-ass family. Probably had something to do with that fucking stunt Bobby pulled. Dumbass is gonna get himself killed. And I'm not gonna bail him out. No fucking way."

Norman listens to Shane.

"Yeah, fine. Whatever. When you see that dumb shit, tell him again what a stupid fuck he is, alright?" Norman hangs up and goes back to his bedroom.

The next morning Jennifer is asleep when he gets up, asleep when he gets out of the shower. He looks at her and rolls his eyes. "Fucking lazy," he whispers to himself. She's still good looking, he thinks. At least she's got that. If not, she'd be out on her ass. Then he opens his closet that's on his side of their bed and takes a box down from the top shelf, takes some cash out and puts it in his pocket.

Over at the department, Rodney and Genero are both at the kitchenette, making coffee, bullshitting. "Good morning gentleman," says Norman. He grabs a mug out of the cabinet and a K-cup and starts to make himself a cup.

"You hear the news?" says Rodney.

"Depends which news," says Norman. He grabs his cup and adds creamer, sits and waits for it to cool. Rodney and Genero are sitting at the small table across from him.

Genero takes a sip of coffee and puts the Styrofoam cups he's drinking out of down on the cheap Formica table.

"Jones and Mitchels, guy is dropping charges against them."

Norman takes a sip. "Oh yeah, I thought he was dead set against them. What happened?"

Rodney smiles. "Not sure, but I think," he says, and he pauses briefly to look around him and make sure no one else is listening nearby, "maybe he found out that the harder he pushes the more likely it'll be that somebody looks into the immigration status of all his family members."

Genero looks up at Rodney. He coughs into his hand. His wheeze is painful on the ears. All those years of menthols have taken their toll. "Can't blame the guy, myself. Doesn't want those elderly parents of his deported."

Norman puts down his coffee on the counter. "I brought in some cash to add to the donations too. Oh well, guess I'll just have to keep it." He chuckles. "What happens with the money I already gave over now that they don't need the lawyers?"

"It stays in the fund," says Genero, "God knows somebody else'll need it sooner or later."

Rodney taps a finger on the side of his mug. "On another issue though, I've been talking to officers about your run for Union President. I'd say it's in the bag, like we always thought. But you know Dan Nichols, right? That he's running against you? Some of the guys, the new guys, you know, they like him. Some of them think you're dirty, is the sense I'm getting."

Norman scoffs, takes a sip from his coffee and looks over at Genero, who shakes his head. "Nichols spreading any of this shit?"

Rodney shrugs. "Could be. Could be. I saw him talking to this real shady lookin' fucker out in the parking lot the other day. Not sure what's up with that."

Putting down the cup, Norman says, "What'd he look like?"

"Muscle-bound ginger."

"That would be Brett Bernauer."

Genaro chimes in. "That's the brother of that girl, right?" Norman picks back up the coffee and nods as he takes a sip. "A real shame the things that girl said about you. That's the thing with these slut-types, I find. It's always been the case, even when I was young. They get in over their heads. Put out. Then they start crying rape and wanting attention. They try to bring a good person's name through the mud. Your dad wouldn't have any of that though, God bless him."

"God bless him," Norman repeats.

They all finish their coffees and leave. Norman sees Dan come out of the locker room and leave the building. He follows him out and to his car. When Dan turns on the engine Norman comes over and knocks on the window.

"How's everything, Danny?"

Dan shuffles some paperwork he has on his passenger seat, doesn't look at Norman. "Fine, you?"

Norman has both his hands on the roof of Dan's cruiser. "You know, I've been better Danny. I've been better."

"Oh yeah," says Dan, "Why is that?" He's looking at his odometer now.

"Well you see, I thought we agreed to run a clean race, but now I'm hearing some people thinking I'm dirty, don't know the specifics, just dirty, and I'm wondering, where'd they get this from?"

Dan looks up at him now. "People form their own opinions, officer Acardi.

Norman looks away. He bites the inside of his mouth. "Yeah, I suppose they do." He bends down, looks at Dan in the eyes, doesn't blink. "I seen your brother around."

"Oh yeah."

"Yeah. He's on the H, I guess. That's bad stuff. Not like I gotta tell you. What's even worse is the people those addicts hang around with. Real criminals. You know, I think you better help your brother clean up, hang with a better crowd. Cuz, you know, if he dies, this department doesn't have the resources to go looking into junkie deaths now."

Dan looks at Norman. They stare at each other for a second, say nothing. Dan rolls up the window and drives away.

~ ~ ~

Back at Norman's house, Jennifer moves from the position she pretended to be sleeping in and goes over to the closet. She takes out the box she saw Norman take down when she was watching him with one eye half open. Inside the box are stacks of hundreds bundled together with rubber bands. "You're a fucking criminal, Norman," she says as she puts the box back.

~ ~ ~

Shane walks up the creaky steps to Bobby's house. He didn't go to Bobby's house as a kid like many of the others did. His mother told him and Dan not to hang around with that boy. As he got older he stopped listening to her. He told his mother he wasn't going to be like his pussy-ass older brother.

Shane knocks on the door and Bobby lets him in. He hands Shane a glass pipe and Shane forgets what he came to tell him. Power Rangers is on TV and they laugh at it. They eat a box of donuts and pass out.

CHAPTER 20

Nate meets Brett at a diner. "Shit, I thought Jersey was nice" he says when they sit down at a booth, "Jeanine watches that Real Housewives garbage. They all have mile long driveways and chandeliers. I didn't know Jersey was the South either. I was driving over here and saw a truck with a confederate flag on the hood. What the hell is that shit? I guess I shouldn't be surprised, we got that in PA too."

Brett shrugs. "Thanks for coming."

"Anything you need. You know that man. Besides, I've always wanted to get on your home turf and try to figure out the mystery that is you."

"Nothing's going to help you figure that out."

They both chuckle.

"Listen," says Nate, over a stack of chocolate chip pancakes, "this is personal man, I know that. And shit, I've known you too long to even bother asking if you wanna back down, but I do have to ask this. You sure you can do this without completely losing your shit and killing the guy?"

Brett has a glass of water, nothing else. "I can do this." He can't bring himself to look Nate in the eyes.

They leave the diner in their own cars, Brett leading the way. They park next to a patch of woods a few blocks away and walk under the cover of night without a word. They've each got a flashlight. Brett's hammer's in his back pocket. There's the sound of crickets, of a dog barking far off. Brett motions with his hand to Nate to slow to a crawl when they're two houses away from Bobby's place. They're looking at all the houses, at the windows, making sure no one is watching. If someone was they'd have to turn around and try it a different night.

At Bobby's place they approach via the driveway. Through a side window, they can see lights flickering from a TV. They come to the wooden fence. The van's showing over the top. Brett helps Nate over and then lifts himself. The ground on the other side is mud, a few patches of grass. Both of them sink down an inch when they land.

There's garbage everywhere, food wrappers, beer cans, apple cores, cardboard boxes. In the middle of the back yard there's an aboveground pool, some sort of Wal-Mart special that's bowing out in spots, with filthy water and floating leaves. On the back of the house, there's a sliding glass door with a crack down the middle. Brett pulls on the door handle and is a little surprised when it starts to move. It's easy going, so far.

He looks at Nate. Nate tilts his head and gives him a look as if to say, *remember what we talked about.* Brett nods and they go in. The place is filthier than the yard. It smells like wet dog, but there are no dogs. When Brett steps in he puts his foot on top of a pool cue and almost goes down. He rolls it away with his foot.

They're in a back room with a pool table in the middle. There's dirty clothes on it scattered amongst 40 ounce bottles with cigarette butts floating in them. Nate shakes his head. Brett keeps his eyes peeled for Bobby, staring for seconds at every spot.

There's the slight sound of the TV they saw flickering from the outside. An infomercial's hawking some carpet cleaning product. Brett follows the sound. Nate follows Brett, steps in something that squishes. Brett turns back and makes wide eyes at him, telling him to not make any noises. To which Nate shrugs and raises his hands at their surroundings.

They enter the front room of the house. The blinds are drawn. The disaster that is the room is only shown a little by the light of the TV. They need their flashlights to get a real look. There are blankets and clothes everywhere, amid the furniture; two old couches and a recliner situated around a coffee table decorated with cigarette burns. It smells like sweat and booze and barf. The flashlight beams display ashtrays, more bottles, a bong, a glass pipe, and porno mags. It takes them a minute to realize there're people there, sleeping alcohol and drug-induced sleeps, snoring up storms. One's on the floor and the others on a couch, sunken down almost to the ground.

Nate shines his light on the guy on the floor. He's a mass of flesh. His gut is hanging out with grayish blue stretch marks visible even in the dim light. Nate looks at Brett, who pauses before he shakes his head no. Nate moves the beam to the body on the couch.

Brett throws the blankets off him, still not waking him. He grabs his shirt and drags him over the arm over the couch, making it creak. His eyes open when his lower back slams to the floor and shakes the house. Brett keeps pulling him, towards the back door where they came in, tearing the t-shirt. Bobby starts to scream and flails his arms until he somehow picks up the pool cue. He swings it and breaks it over Brett's shoulder, to no effect.

Shane opens his eyes and tries to sit up. Nate steps on his chest. "Not so fast, big boy." Shane pulls a cell phone out of his pants pocket and tries to bring it to his face. Nate bends down and slaps it out of his hand. It flies across the room and thuds against a wall. "We're not here for you. You stay calm and we'll be gone. Not a hair on your head'll be harmed."

Brett drags Bobby over the threshold of the back door and into the mud. "Get up, you fuck." Bobby looks up in terror, unable to move, frozen. Brett shakes his head and picks him up by the shirt that's mostly a rag now. He grabs the hair on the back of Bobby's head and walks him over to the pool. "You remember me," says Brett. With the other hand he points to the scar on his face. He dropped his flashlight somewhere in the house. A streetlight nearby makes the scar just barely visible. Bobby nods. His eyes go to the hammer in Brett's pocket. He starts to swing fists and hits Brett in the shoulders.

Nate comes through the back door and says, "Easy, remember what we talked about."

Brett forces Bobby's head into the pool. He's kicking and swinging his arms, trying to push himself up. Shane tries to run at Brett and Nate holds him back with a hand on the collar of his shirt, slipping a bit in the mud, splattering some on the house.

Brett brings Bobby out of the water. There's a leaf on his forehead, dirt up his nose, and a piece of snot hanging off his chin. He's coughing and yelling. Brett sticks him in again. The water is bubbling. Holding his head with one hand, Brett punches him in the kidney with the other.

Shane makes another effort to go at Brett and Nate puts his arm against his chest. He pushes his girth against Nate's forearm and tries to get around him, slides back against the door. His wheezes are audible like a zipper going up and down. "You're gonna kill him, yo. Stop!"

Brett pulls Bobby out. He's coughing and leaning on the white metal frame of the pool until it collapses under his substantial weight. The filthy water comes crashing everywhere. They all fall to the ground, rolling. Bobby kicks Brett in the face. His head jerks back. He does it again. He goes for a third time and Brett catches his foot. He grabs his hammer that's come out of his pocket and landed on the ground next to him. He brings it hard against the side of Bobby's knee and his leg breaks, goes in a direction it was never meant to go. Bobby screams and cries, spitting blood into the air. He tries to kick Brett with the other foot. "You're fucking crazy!"

Shane wipes muddy water from his eyes. Nate's

somewhere on the ground so he can finally charge at Brett. He hits him in the side of his chest with his shoulder, knocking him off of Bobby and onto the ground where the pool used to be. He punches Brett in the forehead, an inefficient sloppy punch that doesn't do much. Brett's not fazed at all.

Nate runs and kicks Shane down, then slips on the wet ground and lands next to him. Getting to his feet after forcing himself up with hands in the mud, he stands over him, knocks him out cold with one punch and watches his chest rise and fall to make sure he didn't kill him.

Brett straddles Bobby and punches him in the head again and again. Bobby's screaming. They're not real words, just animal sounds. Brett keeps punching. The blood keeps flowing and the screams turn to coughs, which turn to gargles, which turn to nothing.

"That's enough," says Nate. He takes a step closer.

Brett punches again. Then he grabs Bobby's head on the sides with both hands and begins slamming his head into the ground.

Nate grabs his shirt and lifts him up. "That's enough man, c'mon."

They both look down at Bobby. His face doesn't look like a face anymore. It's red pulp and bone. His chest isn't rising and falling like Shane's.

Nate lets go of Brett's shirt. "Fuck."

CHAPTER 21

1995

He stopped taking the bus to school soon after it happened to Sarah. His parents pulled her out of the public school, but said they didn't have money for both of them to go to a private school. Plus, he was almost done anyway.

He stopped riding the bus because he didn't want to be around anyone any longer than he had to be. As it was, during the day at school, he had to deal with their stares and their whispers. Until the day before, he still had no idea what they were whispering about, though he knew it had something to do with his sister. He had assumptions, but assuming the truth and knowing it are different.

Kicking bits of broken concrete and pebble as he walked, Brett had his head down when Dan drove up alongside him and asked him if he wanted a ride to school. In the car, Dan started talking about the plans he had for when he graduated. He was going to go to a local state school to study criminal justice, then he'd try to become a local cop. He heard it was a decent way to make a living, to take care of a family, didn't know what else to do. Brett thought the idea was shit, but he liked Dan, enough anyway, so he kept quiet.

Dan asked him what his plans were. At first he shrugged. Then he said he'd just work, get a job doing something. He didn't care.

At one point in the ride Brett asked Dan where his brother Shane was. Dan said his brother was a loser and he wasn't giving any rides to a damn loser no matter how many times his parents told him he had to.

Dan started again on college. Said he hoped to be a walk-on on the baseball team.

Brett looked at him and knew he was speaking, but all he could hear was his conversation with his mother from the other day. She'd come in his room and sat on his bed, started off by saying something had happened to his sister. She continued on with some watered-down details he only half heard. The nerve-endings in his head were firing too fast to comprehend everything. The only words from the conversation that he could solidly recall were his own.

You mean they fucking raped her?!

When the words echoed in his brain again his blood turned hot.

"You alright, man?" said Dan. They were stopped at a traffic light a block away from the school. He looked up at Dan and then around him, outside of the car, like he was surprised at where he was, didn't know how he got there.

"Just tired," Brett answered.

In his English class that day the teacher wanted them to work on admissions essays to college. He told her he wasn't going to college anyway so he shouldn't have to write an essay. She let him sit at a desk in the back with his head down, told him if the principal stopped by the class he had to at least pretend he was working on something. He looked out of a window and stared at the birds. There were cardinals. One was all red and one had some brown. He knew one was male and one was female, but didn't know which was which. The one with brown was building a nest and he thought that no matter how good the nest was something would come along and destroy it.

Dan found him at his locker after the final bell and asked him if he wanted a ride home. Brett said no, said he had something to do. He walked to the abandoned strip mall where Jonathan died and hid behind a dumpster.

Nothing had operated out of the building for a long, long time, so the only thing the dumpster smelled like was old. There was a rusty ladder nearby attached to the building that must have been used when the place was functional for some type of maintenance roof access. He stared at it until night fell and a beat up Firebird pulled up.

Joe was driving. Norman in the passenger seat and Bobby in the back, both holding cases of beer. They were all 21 or older, so Brett wasn't sure what their rationale for drinking there was. Just something losers did.

Behind the dumpster, only visible if they cared to search, he watched as they climbed the ladder. There was a knife in his pocket. A long blade with a shiny wooden-looking handle that he'd taken out of his father's toolbox. His father got it when he earned his Eagle Scout. Brett remembered people telling him how successful Eagle Scouts were supposed to be. Most things that were supposed to be turned out to be shit.

Brett waited another half an hour before he went up. He could hear them laughing even behind the dumpster. He wasn't sure exactly how it would work out, but didn't care as long as somebody bled.

White paint chipped off the ladder as he went up. Reddish brown rubbed off on his fingers from the rust. The sound of a car made him pause midway up. Just somebody turning around.

They didn't see him when he got on the roof. They were at the other side, drunk and shouting. Somebody had brought up a boom box and they were blasting Metallica. Hetfeild's voice was coming through the old speakers, screaming "Sad but True!" There were cans and bottles strewn around. Some from that day, but some undoubtedly from other occasions, left to litter a spot that no one cared about anymore aside from the town's degenerates, criminals, and homeless.

The roof was black tar, rough like sand paper. Brett crouched along, hiding behind an old air conditioning unit. The roof flexed under his feet at spots and he envisioned it collapsing underneath, himself being impaled on some old shelving unit left in whatever abandoned store it was he was walking over.

It occurred to him, with his back against the cold metal of the air conditioning unit, that whatever he was going to do would probably land him in jail. He didn't care. He thought back to the ride to school with Dan and all the talk about plans and thought it was good he didn't have any. They'd be like the bird's nest, destroyed, torn apart by some unforeseen circumstance. He closed his eyes and took a breath, felt the knife handle in his right hand, pushed the dull side against his leg.

He took another look. The three of them formed a triangle. Joe and Bobby were side by side, about three feet apart. Norman was at the center, the furthest from him, but still, the one he wanted.

The knife clenched, he ran out from behind the air conditioner.

Bobby saw him first. "What the fuck?!" He put out his arm and his fist and stepped back.

Joe bent down and ran towards Brett. He dodged the knife and caught Brett in the gut with his shoulder. Brett kept pushing forward, forcing Joe backwards as if he were a defensive lineman on the football field.

Brett swung the knife over Joe's back. He could have lunged it right into the center of his back, or into the side of his neck, but that wasn't what he wanted. His eyes were on Norman. He spat like a rabid animal, kicked Joe in the shins. Joe punched him in the side of the ribs. Immediately, Brett found it hard to breath. Pain raked his chest with each inhale. Joe took him to the ground and kicked the knife out of his hand. It bounced off of the air conditioning unit and landed on the roof.

Joe and Bobby took opposite sides. They both kicked and kicked, breaking more ribs. Brett was screaming, part out of pain, part from rage. The sand paper-like surface of the old roof started to abrade his bare elbows and the back of his head.

Like some sort of TV villain, Norman walked over, laughing, with the knife in his hand, looking at it. "What are you a fucking Boy Scout? Boy Scouts don't try to stab people, you shit."

Bobby and Joe stopped kicking. Brett tried to get up, but the pain was too much. In between painful breaths, he was able to speak. "My sister," he said, spitting blood with every word, "what you did."

Joe spit in his eye. "We didn't do shit to your sister, motherfucker. She wanted that shit, that fucking slut." Bobby laughed. His gut shook as he did and part of it stuck out from under his shirt.

Norman took the knife and stood over Brett. "So you were gonna stick up for your sister, huh?" he said. There was a zit the size of a dime on his chin. "That's real cute."

Joe stood by Brett's head and held his arms. Bobby took his feet. Norman took the knife and carved a line from Brett's eye to his chin, down the center of his right cheek. His faced turned red immediately. Blood streamed down to his neck. The blade felt cold in his face. The cut started to burn only when Norman was done. Brett screamed and cursed.

Norman stood. The others let go of his arms and his legs. Brett cried with his hands over his face and they laughed at him. Norman walked to the side of the roof and threw the knife off the side. They all heard it hit the metal dumpster Brett had hid behind.

"Now look at you," said Norman, "you gotta go everywhere forever with that cut on your face, you ugly fucking pussy." He picked up a beer bottle and took a swig, burped.

Brett rolled onto his stomach. They let him get to his knees.

"Now get the hell out of here," said Joe. "You come looking for trouble again we'll cut your balls off and fuck you like your sister."

Brett crawled to the ladder without looking up. The feeling of humiliation was so immense he thought he'd never look anyone in the eyes ever again. On his way down, he slipped on one of the rungs of the ladder and banged his chin on it, biting off a small piece of his tongue.

He went to the dumpster and got the knife. He wanted to put it back before his father noticed it was gone.

CHAPTER 22

Brett looks down at the dead body of one of the men that raped his sister. As pathetic in death as he was in life. Brett should feel remorse, he realizes. He knows he told Nate he wouldn't do it and that he let him down. For that he does feel bad, but not for killing Bobby. No, his only regret in that regard is that Bobby lived as long as he did.

Nate's pacing back and forth and cursing into the air. Thunder cracks overhead. "You're a real fucking asshole, you know that. You swore to me this shit wouldn't get out of hand. And fuck me too for trusting your crazy ass. Fucking Jeanine always said I should watch you, that one day you'd take shit too far and look, now here we are and what the fuck are we gonna do, man?"

Brett expected to feel better than he does. There's no relief that's supposed to come from vengeance, only worry that the cycle will continue and grow even more out of control until it swallows up him and everyone he cares about. He wants to fall to his knees. He looks at Nate. "I... I'm sorry, man."

"The fuck you are, man, the fuck you are." Every word comes out of Nate's mouth with palpable anger. "But look, I don't wanna hear your damn apologies. Not now. You tell me what we do. What's the plan, big man?" He points at Shane. "And don't forget about this one, a real fucking land whale."

"We dump the body, maybe in the Delaware. We take Shane with us. Make sure he's not saying anything. I know him, he's not so bad."

The sky opens above and heavy rain pelts them. Drops ripple in the mud and the puddles of the yard. "Nah man, no way. Why are we dumping the body? To hide that you did it? From what I know about this place, from what you've told me and from what I've seen, they're gonna know you're involved as soon as he turns up missing. They are coming for you, body or no body. Evidence or no evidence, whether it's legal or not. That'll be a waste of time if you ask me. And what the hell are you talking about, saying we'll take this other guy with us? You gonna torture him? Cut his tongue out or some shit? You're fucking crazier than I thought."

Brett looks at him, expressionless and out of ideas.

Nate looks around. "Let's just get the fuck out of here."

"What? Just leave?"

"Yeah, you were guilty before you even did it. We've got to get you as far away as we can, out of the country or something. We hook up with Jeanine and she'll take care of that shit."

Brett nods. They hop over the fence, Brett taking one final look over his shoulder as he climbs, looking at the damage he created.

In the truck they look at themselves. "We've got to get cleaned up," says Nate. "Imagine getting stopped looking like this."

"We'll go to my parents' place, then we decide from there. Plus, we've got to get Sarah too."

"You gonna get her involved in this?"

"She already is involved. First thing they'll do is go looking for her."

"Fine," says Nate. "She gonna come willingly?"

Brett scoffs. "Probably not."

They pull into the driveway and the sky breaks open. Rain pelts the windshield and they run to the front door. When they open it, covered in filth and gore, Sarah screams, "Jesus, fucking Christ, Brett! What the hell happened?"

She's wearing sweatpants and a tee shirt. Her hair is pulled into a ponytail. Her eyes are puffy as if she was either crying or about to fall asleep.

They both walk in and usher past her. "I'll explain," says Brett. "You're gonna have to pack first." He looks at Nate. "Shower's down the hall. I'll give you some of my clothes that I've got packed."

Sarah is biting her nails. "Who is this?" she says, pointing to Nate, "and what the hell did you do Brett. You look like you killed somebody."

Nate looks at her. "He did."

"What?!"

Brett puts up a hand. "Sarah, this is Nate. He's a friend of mine. He's gonna help us out."

Sarah interrupts. "Brett, what is he talking about? What happened? What did you do?"

Nate starts walking away, towards the bathroom. "I'm gonna get cleaned up."

Sarah pounds on Brett's chest. "What did you do?"

"It wasn't supposed to happen. Just calm down. It was Bobby Reed. He's the one that threw the brick and the note. He has the van... had." He looks down at his hands, shaking, blood and dirt drying now in between the grooves. "I just lost it Sarah. I lost it." His eyes swell with tears.

Sarah puts her head on his chest and punches him in the shoulder. "I told you to leave it. You never listen to me. You never listen to anyone. What are we going to do, Brett? What are we going to do?" Her face is turning red and blotchy.

"I don't know." He holds her, and continues, "They'll come for you, you know that. Fucking Norman. Shit, the police department. You need to go to my place until I figure something out."

Nate comes out of the shower and Brett goes in. Sarah packs. When Brett comes out and starts to pack himself, Sarah isn't speaking to him now that's she's had time to think on the situation. She's looking at him like she intends to strangle him. Once everything is ready to go, she says, "You can never control yourself, can you?" It's something their father would have said.

Brett's head is down. He's feeling the shame like an August sun against his scalp. Then, as if to justify what he's done, he says, "You know that fucking Norman Acardi is a cop? A fucking cop, Sarah! Jennifer Kyle married his stupid ass. You remember her?"

"I really don't care, Brett."

They go outside. Nate's sedan is parked on the street in front of the house. "You can follow behind us," Brett says to him.

"No," says Sarah, "no us. I don't want to ride with you." She walks to the car and opens the passenger side door. Nate looks at Brett with raised eyebrows.

Nate and Sarah drive for two hours in silence. On route 80 Nate starts talking, whether she's listening or not he doesn't know, just can't take the silence anymore. "You're brother's a fucked up dude, that's for sure. I've never met anybody like him, so angry, at almost everything. But I'll tell you this, he has a heart and he cares about you." Her only response is a huff and a shrug as she continues to look at the pouring rain outside her window.

A deer runs across the multi-lane highway and somehow makes it unscathed into the bushes on the eastbound side. They both gawk at the wonder of it. Luck like that is unique.

"Let me tell you what I'm thinking," Nate continues after the bushes shaking in the wake of the frantic deer are well in their rearview. "I got this friend, okay, Jeanine. Me and her are close. Your brother knows her. Look, she's got connections like crazy and I mean the kind of connections that can make shit happen. Jeanine's a paramedic, but she's more than that, alright? She's sees a lot of screwed up shit, shit she isn't okay with. So she tries to help people the best she can, especially people in trouble. You understand?" Sarah turns her head to look at him and nods her head. "You know these domestic violence shelters, right? Well, sometimes they ain't enough. So my girl Jeanine, she can make somebody disappear. I'm talking new name, birth certificate, social security number, whatever. Usually she does it for women escaping men about to kill them, but she'd hook you and Brett up, I'm sure."

Sarah has a finger on the window next to her, tracing a drop of rain that's easing its way down to the door. "Does my brother know about this?"

"Sure. I'm hoping to convince him to go that way. What do you think? You in?"

"I don't know. I guess I don't have all that much I'd be giving up. Let me think about it though."

"Of course. Shit, it's not a light decision. I know that."

They get to Brett's place around midnight. Al's howling gleefully and rubbing on everyone's legs. Fred Donte fed him while Brett was away, and from the girth of Al it looks like he didn't miss a single feeding, maybe even added a few.

Everyone puts down their bags. Sarah assesses her brother's home. "This place is disgusting."

Nate nods in agreement and turns to Brett. "So, again, what's the plan, big man?"

Brett thinks back to a conversation he had years ago with his mother after Jonathan died. The shock was still raw. He didn't want to go to school, didn't want to get out of bed. He told his mother that he didn't know how he was supposed to do anything and she told him to just put one foot in front of the other and keep going. That's as far as his plans went, even now.

He looks out of the back door. The deck light is on and illuminating the still pelting rain. The wind is pushing tree branches sideways. "Let's get some sleep. In the morning, you guys stay here. I'm going back."

131

Nate shakes his head. "You're stupid and crazy, man. Look, I was talking this over with your sister in the car. Jeanine can hook you up. You know that. We make you disappear. Both of you."

Brett looks at his sister, who's still not ready to meet his gaze. "I don't really feel like backing out of this."

"Who gives a fuck," says Nate. "They're going to kill you."

Still looking at the ground, Sarah says, "He's right. They will."

Nate nods. "And your sister can go with you. We can make that happen."

Brett looks again at Sarah, who does nothing to indicate she'd go along. "Let me sleep on it, alright?"

"Okay," says Nate, "Now we're talking some sense."

The rain stops at some point after Nate and Sarah have passed out. The only one awake other than Brett is Al, sniffing and rubbing against the bags and belongings they'd brought in. Sarah's on the futon and Nate's in a sleeping bag on the floor.

Brett picks up the cat and rubs his forehead against his moist nose. He's purring like a motor. He meows once and then clamors to get down. Brett pets him one final time in the center of his head and then grabs the last protein drink from his fridge. He closes the front door behind him as he leaves, softly, so as not to wake either of them, and drives away.

When he parks down the street from Fred Donte's house he gets a pen and a small note pad from the glove box, jots something down under the light of the dashboard and sticks the paper in his pocket. Like he did the day before at Bobby's, he sneaks up to Fred's house with is hammer in his back pocket. Fred might be understanding if he found Brett creeping around his place, but his wife would have a stroke, so he's got to take it slow and careful. There's a motion sensor light that comes on at the side of the house. Brett stands like a statue until it goes out and then progresses on. Thank God Frank's allergic to dogs.

In the backyard he spots the fabled shed. He hasn't seen it before, but Fred's mentioned it many times, said his wife made him get the thing because she doesn't want the shit in the house, bad enough he's got the things anywhere nearby. There's one padlock on it.

Brett's got a duffle bag with him that he puts down next to him and takes out his hammer. He wedges the claw end between the padlock and the wood of the shed. The wood creaks and a bead of sweat pops out on Brett's forehead. He's got to put his foot against the wood to get enough leverage. It feels like he'll crack the door before he gets the lock off. There's a popping sound and the metal falls to the ground. A squeaking sound from the door hinge makes Brett pause before he opens it all the way. Once inside he loads the bag with two rifles, a handgun, and boxes of ammunition.

Before he leaves he takes the crumpled piece of paper out of his pocket and leaves it on the ground, weighted by the broken padlock. On the paper, it says, "Frank, I'm sorry. I hope you understand. – Brett."

CHAPTER 23

A crow sits on a branch above Shane, peering down on him, cawing. Drops of water are falling from the tree after the last night's heavy rain. It's gotten colder. Shane shivers, unconsciously, and rolls onto his side in the mud. The crow squawks again and wakes him up. The first thing he sees is Bobby. His face is unrecognizable.

He rushes to his feet and feels the pain in his head from being punched by Nate. Where the hell did that massive black motherfucker come from? He has to suppress the urge to vomit when he stands over Bobby and gets a full view of the carnage. Inside, his phone is where Nate threw it, broken screen but still functional. The TV is still on, some morning talk show.

Norman doesn't answer when he calls. It's early and he has it off, probably has the phone on silent so his wife doesn't bitch. Shane tries again and again. The thought occurs to him that he should call the regular police line, but as much as Norman runs the show, he doesn't control everything. They'd be obligated to investigate to some degree and God only knows what some new jack officer would pull up. They've got to have some semblance of order and professionalism to keep the state from sticking its nose in the department's affairs. Plus, there's nothing saying his brother wouldn't be the one to respond.

Shane grabs a Coke from the fridge and starts walking to the trailer park. The shakes are everywhere now. It's been a weak since he's scored, not because he's been trying to stay clean, but because everything's dried up. His head is pounding and he's not sure now if it's from the hit or the withdrawal. There's a painful jolt in his stomach so he runs behind somebody's bushes and has diarrhea. Norman still doesn't answer when Shane pulls up his pants and tries to call again. Then the battery on his phone dies and the screen goes black.

~ ~ ~

Norman does call him an hour later and hangs up when it gets to voice mail. Given how many times he's threatened Shane and told him not to call him, he knows it has to be an emergency for the fat junkie to call him so much in so little time. Jennifer comes into the bedroom to tell Norman his bacon and eggs are ready and she sees him on the phone. She smirks and tilts her head.

"Oh, don't you give me that shit, Jen. I've got a lot going on."

As she turns away, she drops a spatula on the ground that she carried over from the kitchen and a piece of egg gets on the carpet. Norman shoots out of bed in boxer shorts and a tee shirt and picks up the spatula. The phone is still in his other hand. She's at the stove turning off the burner and he throws the spatula at her. It crashes against the wall. Grease flies from it and gets in her eye.

"You know I'm a fucking cop, right. I mean my job doesn't stop because you want some story-book relationship."

She takes the pan of scrambled eggs and throws them to the ground at his feet. "What you spend your time on has nothing to do with work!" She runs passed him, quickly, dodging his reach, and goes into the bedroom and opens a closet. Pushing folded clothes away stacked on a shelf, she pulls out the shoebox she found and throws it to the floor. The stacks of money come tumbling out. "Tell me what that is!"

"It's none of your fucking business is what it is!"

She starts kicking the money with her bare feet. "You're a criminal you piece of shit! Tell me where it came from!"

He glances down at his cell phone to make sure he hasn't missed another call from Shane and she catches him. She tries to swipe the phone out of his hand.

"Pay attention to me, Norman! Who are you talking to?"

He catches her wrist with his left hand, drops the phone, and slaps her across the face, splitting her lip and spinning her onto the ground. She's crying and he steps over her, puts on clothes, packs a uniform into a bag, and leaves her there, leaves the house.

Officer Pete Waxman is leaving the station when Norman comes walking up. "I thought you were off today?"

Norman is looking at the ground. "Gonna see if there's some overtime, you got a problem with that?"

Waxman lets the door close behind him, doesn't bother holding it open for Norman. "No problem, no. Just thought a man with your multiple lines of income wouldn't need overtime."

Norman stops and looks up. "What the fuck are you talking about?"

"Some things I heard on the street, that's all. I mean, I don't have any proof, so don't get your panties in a bunch, but one thing I've learned from my time is that when you start hearing something from multiple different sources, that's time you start believing it."

Norman shakes his head and opens the door. "I don't know what you're talking about."

In the locker room, as Norman is changing, Rodney comes from behind and puts a hand on his shoulder. Norman just about shoots into the ceiling.

"You alright there, pal?" says Rodney. He's got his uniform shirt draped over his arm.

"Yeah, you know. This place sometimes. Had the pleasure of seeing Waxman on my way out. High and mighty sonofabitch, thinks he and Nichols are going to clean this place up. He's calling me dirty. That piece of garbage."

Rodney sits on the bench next to him. "Ignore that guy. He don't know shit. But we gotta clean up, that's my thinking. Your boys are too sloppy. Shane and those townies. Why d'you think Waxman thinks you're dirty? Cause you've got a known history with all that white trash, Norm."

Norman's got fire in his eyes. "Oh, and we bring in your goons from Brooklyn and no one's gonna make that connection, right?"

"My guys'll be smart about it at least. Won't walk around town high on their own supply, like that fat shit. And goddamn Norman, he's Nichols's brother. I mean that's just not smart."

Norman stands up and backs Rodney into the lockers. He jams his elbow into his throat. Rodney's gasping. "You listen you piece of shit, these are the people I trust. I'm in charge. This is my operation. None of this shit would happen if it wasn't for me. You understand? I had the balls to get this up and going. You don't know shit, so you keep your mouth shut."

~ ~ ~

On the other side of town, Shane finally reaches Joe's trailer. Inside, he and his brother Kenny are asleep. Shane starts shouting. "They killed him, you guys. They killed him!"

Joe wakes up. He's on the couch in his underwear, a beer stain on his white T-shirt, no blankets on him despite the cold and the lack of heat in the trailer. Kenny is asleep in a recliner with a pizza box at his feet.

"Killed who?" says Joe.

Shane looks at his phone again. "Bobby. They beat him so bad they fucking killed him."

"Quiet your fucking mouth," says Joe. "Who did?"

"Bernauer and some black guy."

~ ~ ~

As the day becomes the evening, Jennifer drives around Madison Park, not sure where to go, too frightened to go home. Before she left, she packed some bags with clothes and blankets. Her parents moved to Florida years ago so she can't go stay with them. All her friends she grew up with got the hell out of dodge too. Nowhere to go, she'll sleep in her car until she figures it out.

She's watched documentaries before about the Mafia, about the guy they based Goodfellas off of and some of the others. They talk about the wives on those things too. If they knew about the things their husbands were doing and didn't do anything or didn't tell anybody then they're just as much up shits creek.

She pulls into an abandoned lot and stares at the rubble of a building in front of her. She remembers hearing a rumor she dismissed at the time about Norman raping that Bernauer girl behind the building and wonders now, as she runs her hand against her sore lip, if there was any truth to it.

CHAPTER 24

1995

Unlike his sister, who used the back door to escape their parents after her incident with Norman Acardi and his friends, Brett came in through the front door. With a bloodied face and broken ribs, he was in too much pain to even wonder how they would react let alone determine a strategy to avoid them. With blood seeping through the fingers he held to his face, he told them to leave him alone. It was a miracle the knife didn't poke through the other side of his cheek and into his mouth.

His mother shrieked and demanded he go to the hospital. His father wanted to know who did it to him. Of course he guessed the correct answer, that the people who did it to him where the same people behind the family's other tragedies. They both agreed he was an idiot for openly confronting them. Brett ignored their scolding and got into the shower. He washed off the grime that stuck to his skin from the rooftop and watched his blood go down the drain in a red swirl. When he dried off he went and stuck the knife back in his father's toolbox.

In the end, Brett was able to convince them not to take him to the hospital or to contact the police, but to instead take him to an urgent-care center to get stitched. "Unfortunately, young man," said the doctor who sewed him up, "you're going to have this scar for the rest of your life." He left the place with thick black stitches running down his face and a pocket full of pain pills. Neither of his parents looked at him.

Graduating from high school a few weeks later, Brett

still couldn't take a full breath when he stepped on the stage to accept his diploma. There's nothing you can do for broken ribs, the people at the urgent-care center said to him and his parents, only time can heal them. They were still sore when he started working for a local construction company cleaning out gutters the next month. At 18 he still wasn't able to grow any facial hair, so the full length of the pink scar was out in full force and visible to all.

Sarah had three years still before she graduated from the all-girls high school she was going to, but it wasn't clear to anyone that she would be able to finish. She sat in the back of all her classes and slept or drew in a notebook. She had open confrontations with her teachers and other students. The principal called home on multiple occasions and said she was difficult. No one knew what to do. They had to send her there, even as expensive as it was. Public school wasn't an option as far as her parents were concerned, not while people were still talking about her and what they thought *she* had done. They tried sending her to a therapist. She'd either lie and say she was fine or say nothing at all.

Things continued to roll downhill. The moving company Joseph worked for was hurting, more competition and less business. They laid him off. He tried to explain things to the bank, but they continued to pursue foreclosure. Other bills were behind too. Their lights were shut off on many occasions, often for more than a week at a time. Brett read Stephen King novels at night with a flashlight. He tried to help his parents as much as he could, but eight dollars an hour pulling leaves and twigs out of people's gutters didn't help much.

Barbara took a job working the drive-thru at a McDonalds down the road. That too didn't help entirely. She was able to bring home free Big Macs though, and everyone enjoyed that, at least when they had the power to microwave them.

It was on a Saturday in July, when his mother had taken Sarah to a therapist appointment, that Brett walked in to his parents' bedroom to ask his father if he could borrow his bike when he saw him put the 9mm to his temple and pull the trigger. The door was open a hair so he didn't knock. There stood his father, finger already pulling the trigger when he walked in. They made eye contact for a split second before the shot rang and the blood splattered on the wall.

Sarah and Barbara found Brett upstairs, frozen and in a ball, next to his father. Brett never touched the gun. Murder was never entertained. Everyone knew it was suicide. There wasn't a note. The payout on the life insurance policy Joseph had taken out before Jonathan died was enough to pay for what was left of the mortgage. A provision changed in most policies meant that, given he'd had the policy for over a decade, the family could still get the money even though he killed himself. At least there was that.

The house and the surrounding town became a place of death to Brett. Barbara tried to get him to go to therapy, the same person Sarah saw, said that after seeing something like that he had to talk to somebody about how he felt. Brett was a legal adult and said to his mother that nobody could force him to do anything. And talking never helped anybody.

For two years he worked as hard as he could. What he didn't spend helping his mother with any bills that the life insurance money couldn't cover, he squirrelled away. Then he took it and bought the cabin in Pennsylvania. Telling his mother and his sister about the purchase and about moving away, he told them he'd still be around, would visit as often as possible. The first year up there he didn't visit once.

Barbara sulked about his leaving, but she didn't cry, all her tears were spent. As much as it pained her, she understood. Everyone around her died, why would anyone want to stay? Like her son, she worked every hour she could.

Sarah did eventually finish high school, by the skin of her teeth. She had no prospects for college or for anything else. She had a friend that graduated a year ahead of her and moved to Brooklyn, so she decided to move in with her.

CHAPTER 25

Brett drives out of Pennsylvania thinking about being a murderer. It's an exclusive club, not one he thought he'd ever enter, even as violent as he was. He always thought he'd be able to stop himself. Vigilante, that club he was proud to be part of. This one, not so much.

His murder was justified. But then, doesn't everyone say that about the things they've done, that they had no other choice? There's no way he can continue down this line of thought and not get bogged down in self-loathing, he decides. More needs to be done.

They're coming, that much is for sure. Joe and Kenny, Norman, maybe others, the police, people that believe in Norman's brand of justice. It's Brett's responsibility to stop them. They can't get to Sarah. And, it's about more than that. They have to pay for what they did.

He pieces together a plan while he drives. Then, getting closer to home, he begins to collect his supplies. First, coffee. Lots of it. Boxes of it. Already brewed from Dunkin Donuts. He'll be waiting for them for as long as it takes and can't fall asleep. Then, bandages, heavy ones like after a woman gives birth, and pain killers, bottles of them, and pairs of scissors and tweezers, all from a medical supply store. It'll be bloody, he knows that much, and most likely it'll be bloody for him. Finally, ply wood, duct tape, and another flashlight since his last one busted in the fight with Bobby.

Back at the house, he covers every entrance but the front door with the plywood, nails it down. He wants to control how they come at him. He covers most of the windows too. At the front door, he's positioned a table on its side nearby, to hide behind. It's the kitchen table, thick wood. It won't stop a bullet, but it'll slow one down. The duffle bag is filled with guns and medical supplies.

When he first sits down behind the overturned table, it's two in the afternoon and he sits there for hours, trying to be patient. It's always been hard for him to control his thoughts, and it is now more than ever. They fall to suicide. To his father. He looks down at the bag of guns. At the handgun. There's no way he can escape the sound he heard that day.

It would be so easy to end it, to put the end of one of those guns in his mouth and pull the trigger, just like his old man did. Somebody'd come in a day or so and scrape him off the wall and that would be that.

The sun starts to fall and he wishes he was back at his cabin with Nate and Sarah. He wishes he knew how to have a good time. To relax and be comfortable around other people. But it's too late now. No matter how it ends, it'll end.

The Oldsmobile pulls up a few houses away, on the opposite side of the street. It's squealing until the squealing stops and two bodies emerge. Brett gapes at them through the window. It's the same two he saw at his mother's funeral, looking at him and his sister. One's taller and has on a black T-shirt and blue work pants - Joe. The other's closer to the ground and wider, has a mullet and is wearing a wife-beater and identical blue work pants – Kenny. They've both got cigarettes hanging out of their mouths.

Kenny carries a rifle in both hands, loads it as he walks. As he gets closer Brett sees a handgun wedged in his belt. He keeps coming straight at the house, right where Brett wants them. Joe, who carries a shotgun and barks the orders at Kenny, goes around to the back of the house. They walk with heavy feet and long, slow strides. They both stumble; drunk or high or both.

Kenny doesn't go right to the front door. He pulls a

hunting knife from the back of his pants and starts slashing the tires on Brett's truck. All four of them go flat.

Out of the corner of his eye Brett scans the neighborhood to see if anyone is watching. After seeing no one he leaves the one window he didn't board up and runs behind the table, aims a rifle where he thinks a head is about to appear.

The knob shakes. There's a rattle sound from the outside. At the back of the house, the glass of the sliding door shatters. Joe starts to bang against the plywood. It sounds like he's throwing his body at it. The front door is shaking and Brett's watching it crack. He can see Kenny's boot coming through. Then the wood around the latch comes loose and the door swings open. The end of a gun enters first. Brett aims and fires. The recoil's stronger than he thought it would be. He hits nothing. Kenny shows his face and fires. A bullet wizzes passed Brett and makes powder of the sheetrock wall behind him.

Brett fires again. It's a wild shot. The bullet flies into the hood of the Oldsmobile. He shoots again and again it hits the car. Kenny peaks his head around the entrance way and shoots. The bullet hits Brett in the trapezius muscle between his shoulder and his neck. It tears through his shirt and rips off a piece of flesh.

The banging at the back of the house continues. Brett pops up from behind the table and returns fire. A string of blood comes from Kenny's neck and he falls back. Brett hurdles the table and goes towards the door. Kenny's at the bottom of the front steps getting back to his feet when Brett fires again and hits him in the chest. There's a shotgun blast at the back of the house followed by the sound of Joe making his way inside.

Brett bounds down the stairs, dropping his rifle and pulling a handgun from his pocket. Blood is running down his chest and soaking through his shirt. He kicks the rifle from Kenny's hand and pistol-whips him in the eye. Kenny goes for the handgun at his waist and Brett steps on his hand, breaks his wrist and the bones of his hand. He brings Kenny to his feet and puts the gun to his head. "Get up the stairs." Then he grabs the gun from Kenny's belt and flings it to the ground.

Back inside, Joe's got the shotgun pointed, pumped, and ready to go. "Put it down or I put a bullet in your brother's head," says Brett. He's positioned Kenny's body in front of him.

Joe closes one eye and rests his cheek against the barrel. "Fuck you."

By the time the blast rings out, Brett's on the ground, crawling to the kitchen to his right. When he looks up he sees Kenny get his face blown off. The front room is painted red. Behind a kitchen cabinet, on his ass, Brett turns and pulls the trigger. Joe screams. The shotgun falls to the ground. The bullet caught him in the arm, on the inside of the elbow. Brett rolls onto his gut and aims the handgun. Fires. Fires again.

Joe's on the ground with a wound in his thigh and one in his chest, in addition to the one in his arm. Brett walks to him and puts the metal to his forehead. "Tell me what you did to my sister, you fuck."

Joe spits blood into the air. "Didn't do shit."

Brett shakes his head. "You should have never been born." He pulls the trigger.

The lights are on in the neighboring houses. They're calling the police. With the duffle bag over his shoulder, Brett starts to run through people's yards, hopping fences and running from dogs. Sirens start to blare. The police lights are reflecting off of every surface.

One yard he runs through has a high wooden fence. He tries to hoist himself above but falters and falls to the wet ground. A black dog comes running towards him. Quickly, he tries again to get over, but the dog bites his foot and pulls. Brett can feel teeth through the fabric of his boot. They pierce his flesh and he screams. He hits the dog on the head with the heavy bag while still holding onto the fence with one arm. Lights turn on in the house and somebody, a male, starts yelling. A young boy peers out of the window. The dog starts shaking its head with its teeth still deep into Brett's foot. He can feel the skin and the muscle tear. He twists the bag around and pulls out his hammer. There's a crunch and a whimper when he smashes it against the side of the dog's face. The animal falls to the ground and part of the sole of Brett's boot goes with it. The boy pounds against the window and a man comes out to the backyard with a cell phone in his hand just as Brett makes it over the fence.

A few more houses and he's at a major road. Some businesses there. There're alleyways and dumpsters he can hide behind. Behind a drug store there's enough light from the road for Brett to assess his wounds. He puts down the bag and starts to take things out. Should he keep running? No. He needs to fix himself as much as he can. If they find him, they find him. He'll go down fighting.

The duct tape holds his boot together. The bandages cover his wounds as much as possible. There's a bullet fragment in his shoulder that he pulls out with tweezers. He swallows a bunch of painkillers he packed, not sure how many. Then he starts running.

At the old shopping center there's a car. There are blankets and pillows against the window. Somebody's asleep in it. Brett gets closer. He looks in the window. It's Jennifer.

She opens her eyes when he opens the driver's side door and puts the handgun to her head.

CHAPTER 26

By the time Nate and Sarah wake to the sound of Al knocking over an empty bottle of protein shake that Brett left on the kitchen counter, it's nearly noon. Neither of them seeing Brett or hearing him around, they get up with sleepy eyes and hair to find that not only is he gone, but so is his truck. Nate fumbles through his belongings for his phone and pounds the contact tab for Brett.

When he shakes his head and puts the phone down Sarah says, "Did you really think he was going to answer?" Nate raises his hands in a gesture of acquiescence. "I should have known he'd pull something like this."

"You know where he went, right?"

"He's either going to kill the rest of them or they're going to kill him."

"Exactly what I was thinking. What do you wanna do? I know what I wanna do. I wanna go after his ass and try to stop him from getting himself killed, but I gotta watch out for you too. So tell me what you wanna do." A strong wind blows and water from the previous night's rain comes down from the trees and hits the cabin windows.

Al's sticking near Nate and rubbing against his leg, purring, oblivious to everything going on around him. Sarah's pacing and pulling her hair back into a ponytail. She snaps a hair tie in her fingers and throws it on the ground with a grunt similar to one her brother would make. "Is that the impression my brother gave you? That I need to be protected?" She bites her bottom lip and shakes her head. Without the hair tie her hair spreads in front of her face and she brushes it out of the way. "I don't need anybody to watch out for me, you understand? You do what you want to do. I can take care of myself. You can fucking trust me on that, okay?"

Nate rubs his forehead with his hand and cringes. "Look, that's not what I meant. It came out wrong. Brett never gave me that impression. He never said much about his family one way or the other."

She scoffs. "That's a surprise."

Nate lets out a deep breath. "I just meant it's better if we stick together. In this sort of situation. I'd rather be with somebody else. I should've said it that way. But look, you thought at all about what we talked about on the ride up? You can disappear, put all this shit behind you. I can hook you up with my contact and then you're gone. Once I get you over to her, I go and see what I can do about your brother. See if I can get him off his warpath. No easy feat, as I'm sure you know."

"You have no idea."

"Oh, I think I do actually." Nate bends down to pick up the cat. He rocks Al in his arms like he's a baby. "But seriously though, you think about it?"

"I did"

"And?"

"And I want to go back with you to find him. He's a pyscho, but... But, he's still my brother. Maybe we can get him. I don't know. We'll have to drag him kicking and screaming, but once we get him out of there we can both see this woman and disappear."

"You think he'd want that?"

"I could really care less what he wants at this point."

Nate feeds Al and Sarah loads up the car again. She notices damage from some sort of accident on the passenger side. Rolls her eyes. God knows what type of shit Brett and his friend get up to.

The car bucks as they go up one of the many hills on the back roads leaving Brett's cabin. It feels like the transmission has its own ideas about their trip back and wants out. Sarah puts her hands on the dash. "You're a mechanic?"

Nate laughs, gets the point of why she's asking. He nods. "This beater's been through a lot, but I know she can take it. Don't worry."

There's no bucking when they come to the downward slope of the hill. If only everything was downhill. Sarah smirks at the thought. "So how do you know him?"

"Friends from the gym."

A rumble vibrates out from somewhere under the hood, makes the doors hum. She closes her eyes for a brief second in a way to bite her tongue and stop herself from making another comment about the car. "Friends from the gym." She lets the fact sink in, then asks, "And you just help him kill people?"

They turn onto the highway. The faster speed has the car rumbling more. "Not like that. I didn't know that shit was gonna go down the way it did. You gotta understand that. But yeah, we done stuff like that before. Just never got to that point."

"So tell me really then, how do you know him?"

"Like I said, we're friends from the gym. And, you know, I've helped him with his truck."

"So you're the reason that thing's still on the road?"

Nate looks at Sarah and smiles. "That's right." They stop talking for a minute and look at the road. It's shaping up to be a nice day. The sun is announcing itself from behind patches of clouds that owned the day before. The sound of tires on pavement is hypnotic. "But to get at what I think you want to know, we do some things together. This friend of mine, the woman I mentioned to you before, she lets us know about people that need help. So we help them. That's it."

Sarah thinks she sees a tiny ribbon of smoke peak out

from the front of the car. She tells herself she didn't. Pulling her cell phone from her pocket she calls Brett again and then puts it down on her lap with a sigh of frustration when he doesn't answer. "How do you help people?"

"We make their problems go away."

She pulls in her bottom lip a little. The ribbon of smoke pops out to say hello again and this time it's followed by a friend. "Yeah, I think I know what you mean. Does anybody *ask* you to make their problems go away?" Nate doesn't answer. He pulls the car to the right. The bouncing on the rumble strip before they get to the shoulder makes Sarah's teeth shake.

"What's the problem?"

"She's thirsty." He gets out of the car and goes to the trunk. Sarah watches as he goes to the front with a gallon jug of water and a bottle of transmission fluid. He gets back in and they pull off.

"You sure this car can take all this?"

"Didn't really plan on doing this much." Then, as soon as they get across the Delaware River out of Pennsylvania, right around the time Brett is hiding himself behind the kitchen table to wait for Joe and Kenny, they hit a wall of traffic. "Motherfuck this. I swear, Jersey is the worst place on earth to drive."

For an hour they sit and move only inches. They crane their heads out the windows to see what's ahead but their views are obscured by cars and tractor-trailers. The whole car is shaking now. Nate gets out right in the middle of traffic at one point and gives it more to drink. The thing starts to billow like a chimney. It jostles them once more like a death rattle and gives up, stalls right in the lane and won't turn over. Sarah steers and Nate pushes it to the shoulder. Nobody offers to help, they just roll up a few feet once the car is out of the way.

Nate retrieves a toolbox from the trunk and goes under

the hood. Sarah asks him how long it'll take and he shrugs, obviously embarrassed and frustrated. She alternates between standing by him at the side of the car, watching the cars slowly go by, and sitting anxiously inside, drumming her fingers on her knee and trying to reach her brother. There's nothing she can do but be eaten by her anxiety and worry. When she runs her hands through her hair strands come out. She mindlessly opens the glove compartment and sees, under the car's registration and insurance information, a shiny black handgun. Peaking up to look through the windshield, she sees Nate's still under the car, so she takes out the gun, likes the weight of it in her grip. She dated a guy once who showed her how to us one, brought her to the range a few times. She wonders if she can still do it.

Two more hours go by of Nate cursing under the car until he comes out sweaty with black grease on his brow and chin. The car turns over and he pounds on the gas without a word.

Night's fallen by the time they reach Madison Park. Sarah's about ready to shit kittens as they pull off the Turnpike. She bites her fist when they near the house and see police lights. "Oh Jesus, Brett. What did you do?" The house is surrounded by ambulances and cop cars. A medic pushes a stretcher with a body on it covered with a sheet across the street. The house is cordoned off by police tape. Sarah sees a cop and rolls down the window. "Danny! Danny! What happened? Is that Brett? Please Danny, tell me that's not Brett."

Dan comes over to the car. There's a cop behind him watching him, looking at Sarah and Nate. Sarah's never seen the guy before. He's built like a brick shit house and covered in tattoos. The look on his face is no good, like he's sniffing around for trouble. Dan rests his hands on the car; one gently brushes Sarah's fingers as a sign of sympathy.

"No, that's not Brett, Sarah. But I got to tell you, it looks like he's responsible for this, okay. You oughta get out of here." He bends down to get a look at Nate, nods a hello.

"Where is he?"

"I don't know. They had a line on him for a while. People were calling in. He's on foot. He was running through people's yards. They lost him a few minutes ago. Anybody's guess as to where he's at now."

Nate looks over. "They're gonna kill him."

Sarah's head turns quickly from Dan to Nate and then back. Out of the corner of her eye she still sees the other officer watching and wonders if he doesn't have anything better to do. In a lower voice, she says, "You gotta do something. Can you get to him first? Arrest him at least."

"I will do my best. That is all I can promise you. You know that. But I'm only gonna say it one more time, you need to get out of here, now."

They roll up the windows and turn the car around in the other direction. Before Nate gets off the street, Sarah tells him to stop and turn the car around again so that it's facing the house and all the cop cars. "Watch that guy we were just talking to. When he leaves, follow."

CHAPTER 27

Rodney leaves the scene with a number of other officers to help in the search for Brett Bernauer. He's in his own cruiser by himself. There's no interest for him staying at the scene, collecting evidence and figuring out what happened. That's not what he's made for, the slow patient police work. No, he's meant for chases, for beating down suspects, and for breaking people. Who cares about the evidence anyway? They know who did it.

Rodney's flying. They've lost Bernauer. The fucker was running through yards and people's fences. They got a call he hit somebody's dog with a hammer. Rodney went in the vicinity of that house, talked to the homeowners real quick, but no sign of Bernauer. Officers are driving around everywhere now, shining lights on anything that moves and on most things that don't.

He's a block away from the drugstore, unaware that he's so close to Bernauer. And he scores. It's not Brett. Better than that. Somebody that can give him some answers as to what's going on and who knows what. He can spot that fat fuck a mile away, even in the dark.

The tires screech when he pulls up next to Shane. The junkie nearly falls over he's so startled. "Get in the fucking car," says Rodney, so fast like it's all one word. Shane doesn't have time to think. He just does what he's told. Rodney drives to a gas station that's closed and pulls into the parking lot. He shuts off the car and turns around to look at Shane.

"What the hell is this about? This guy competition or some shit? He from the Mexicans down in Philly?"

Shane looks at Rodney like the guy's out of his mind. It

takes him a second to realize what he's talking about. "Nah, man. It ain't like that. This shit is personal. Like some shit from when we were kids. You wouldn't know."

"Your brother knows them? The guy who did it and his family. I saw him talking to them in front of the house. He seems friendly with them. He got something to do with this?"

Shane pauses for a second like his body is frozen in ice, his brain too. Then he shakes his head and opens his eyes wide. "Nah, Dan's got nothing to do with this man. He was friends with them back like twenty years ago. Fuckin Bernauer's only friend ever was my brother. But that was way back. Dan's just doing his job man."

Rodney looks at Shane with one eyebrow raised higher than the other. Norman told him many times not to completely trust the fat shit. He's a junkie, you can never trust them. Plus, however much he tries to mask it, he's still got some sort of allegiance to his brother. He pulls the latch on the driver's side door and pushes it open with his foot. Shane doesn't even realize Rodney's out of the car until the guy drags him out onto the pavement by his sweatshirt.

Rodney drops Shane onto the ground and steps on his chest. He bends down over his face. "That fuckin brother of yours, he knows, doesn't he? That's what this is about?"

Shane has his hands in front of his face. "I don't know what the hell you're fuckin talkin' about, bro. Like I said, this is personal. Dan doesn't know shit. You think if Dan knew that this is how he'd handle it? Killing the people involved? Not my brother man. He's by the book. Shit, you know that."

Rodney takes his foot from Shane's chest and stands up straight. What Shane's saying makes sense. But then he considers what Shane would have to gain from it all. His brother would take over. He'd probably get a bigger share. No more abuse from Norman. Then Rodney remembers another detail. He bends down again to look at Shane in his bloodshot druggie eyes. "Who's the black guy?"

Shane looks up at the dark sky. Worry crosses his face. All of a sudden it's hard for him to breath. "What black guy?"

"Some fuckin black dude, ridin' around with a white chick, Bernauer's sister. That's what your brother said. I saw him talkin' to both of them."

Shane is silent long enough for Rodney to believe he's holding something back. He punches him in the gut so hard it reverberates throughout his body. Shane's wheezing and coughing. He tries to roll on to his side, but Rodney pins him down with his hands.

"Who's the fuckin nigger, you dumb piece of shit?" Rodney says, right into Shane's greying face.

In between labored breaths, Shane says, "Somebody that works with Bernauer, I think. Something like that." He coughs and turns his head to spit. His hands are shaking. He takes one hand and rubs his shoulder with it, then the back of his neck. He's sweating considerably. "There was a black guy with Bernauer when he killed Bobby. I didn't get his name. Too busy trying... to stay alive."

Rodney narrows his eyes and takes his hands off of Shane. It's obvious to him what's happening to Shane and as long as he plays his cards right it couldn't be more convenient. Take care of the fat boy and then take care of everything else, starting with his brother. "Get in the car," he says to Shane.

Shane takes a full five minutes to get into the car, crawling on the ground, stopping to throw up, holding his chest the whole time. When he gets into the back seat his lungs sound like a broken radiator. "Something's wrong, Rod. Something's... I gotta go to the fuckin hospital."

Rodney starts the engine and drives off. Through the rearview mirror, Shane is purple. Rodney half smiles. "I'll take care of you pal, don't worry."

By the time he gets to the back of the abandoned grocery store where Brett encountered Jennifer, they've already left. Shane looks with one open eye through the window. "Why are we stopping? This ain't no fucking hospital."

Rodney takes his cell phone off of the passenger seat next to him and turns off the engine. He cringes when Shane starts to scream. Then he gets out of the car and locks all the doors. A few steps away, under a street light, he watches the car shake for a few minutes. Shane kicks at one of the windows a few times and cracks it straight down the middle. Rodney shakes his head at that. He'll have to think of some way to explain it, but no biggie. Kids are always hurling rocks and shit at cop cars.

The car stops shaking and he waits another five minutes, smokes a cigarette and then drops the butt in a puddle. Shane is stuffed onto the floor of the back seat. He must have fallen there in his struggle. Rodney looks at his chest and then reaches in to check the pulse on his neck. Nothing. Good.

It's near impossible to push Shane's corpse out of the car. Rodney turns purple and thinks he's about to have a heart attack himself before finally getting him onto the pavement. The body looks like a heap of garbage as he looks back at it driving away. Somebody'll find it when the sun comes up. Nobody'll care much about another dead junkie.

On the road, Rodney calls Norman. "You hear?"

Norman sounds pissed, like he's grinding his teeth. "About what? Fucking Bernauer and Joe? Yeah I heard. Find him and deal with him will you?"

"I'm working on it, alright, but listen. I think Nichols is in on this."

Norman grunts. "You don't stop, do you?"

"Now listen, alright, I'm telling you, there's something

to this. I'm at the house with Nichols and Bernauer's sister and some black guy pull up. Nichols walks over, talks to them like he's their best friend, then he lets them go. I ask him why he did that and he tells me they've got nothing to do with this. Then, now listen to this, I see Shane and I ask about this black guy and Shane tells me this same guy was with Bernauer when he killed Joe. I'm telling you Norm, something's up."

There's silence on the line. Norman groans as if he's considering the facts as Rodney has laid them out. "Bernauer's a crazy motherfucker, I'll give you that. Maybe his sister and this guy are with him, but I don't see the connection to us. You've got nothing to be all paranoid about. Just calm the fuck down. We'll deal with this shit." There's a click on the line that interrupts Norman. "Shit. That's Jennifer on the other line. She ran out on me earlier, pissed about some shit. I gotta go. She's probably got a flat or something."

CHAPTER 28

Brett is standing in the abandoned lot inside the gates of the old Ford plant with a gun against Jennifer's head. No matter how hard he's tried to convince her he won't hurt her, she doesn't believe him. No matter how gentle his grip is on her, he still has the cold metal barrel of a gun pressed to her temple.

It's cold in the parking lot. Wind is howling through the old factory. The air is filled with the smell of rusted metal. The darkness of the sky is starting to lessen. It will be morning soon and all of this will be over, one way or another.

Inside the gates of the plant, it's like the workers went home at the end of their shifts expecting to come in the next day. Instead they got their pink slips and never came back. Vehicles spat off the production lines in the 90's fill the lot with temporary plates still hanging from their bumpers. Many of them look like they'd been lived in at one time or another by homeless. They're filled with blankets and overflowing black garbage bags. There are tow trucks and car-carriers with Styrofoam coffee cups still wedged between windshields and dashboards.

Brett's not saying anything. He's not threatening Jennifer with words. He's calm almost. Certain.

They see headlights. Brett's chest is pushed against Jennifer's back and he can feel her heart pounding. She's shivering, but she's sweating too.

~ ~ ~

Rodney's blocks away from the empty lot where he left Shane's corpse, pulled to the side of the road across from a boarded up house contemplating his next move when his

163

phone vibrates. He's looking at himself in the rearview mirror when he answers. "What's up?"

Norman tells him about the call he just got from Jennifer, tells him not to talk about it over the radio, says they need to handle this on their own, their way, without the rest of the department.

Rodney flattens a strand of hair that's sticking up. "Sure thing."

~ ~ ~

Tears are running from Jennifer's face and onto Brett. The hand that's not holding the gun to her head is on her throat. It isn't choking her, just holding her, but the grip's tight enough for Brett to feel her carotid artery pounding like a runaway train against its rails. He can't see her face, he's staring hard at Norman, but he knows her makeup is streaking like he's seen his sister's do so many times.

Norman puts his gun on the ground and raises his hands into the air. He pushes the weapon a few feet away with his foot. "You're fucking sick Bernauer." There is a snarl to his face when he speaks. The acne scars glisten with sweat under the old yellow streetlights. A few hairs stand up of all those slicked back against his head. "What the hell could you possibly want to do this shit for?"

Brett is shaking with anger. "I want to hear you say it. I want you to say it out loud so your wife hears it. I want you to tell her what you did to my sister. You fuck, you go through your life without any consequences, but not anymore. I want you to say it." As he speaks he shakes Jennifer by her neck and she gags. Her hair flies into his face and he lets it fall without brushing it away.

Norman shakes his head. There's a bulge in his pocket that Brett notices. "You're outta your fucking mind Brett. Your sister made that shit up. She was a damn whore. Your whole family was wrong, you know that. All you guys were nuts from the beginning and none of that's my fault. People like you like to blame everything that's gone wrong in their life on everybody else. I ain't admitting to some shit I never did. And look at you, you come back here and you start killing people. You're the one with the problems, not me."

Jennifer starts to speak. Brett can feel the vibration of it in his hand. "Please Norman, just do what he wants. Please. Please."

Norman's expression doesn't change. His eyes are moving across the lot, scanning behind Brett and Jennifer. Brett turns quickly to look with the gun still pressed to her head. When he looks back at Norman he notices he's taken a step forward. "If you have somebody else coming I will blow her fucking head off and then yours."

"You're not gonna hurt her, Brett. I know that. C'mon. Look at you, you still got that scar on your face. You remember when you got that? I sure as shit do. You're the same damn pussy you always were. Listen, why don't you let her go and try to come at me again."

"Norman please," cries Jennifer, "please help me." Brett can't stand it. Nothing is working out the way he wanted it to. He could put a bullet in her brain and the son of a bitch might not even flinch. She's trembling like a leaf. With his hand that's still around her throat, Brett takes his thumb and gently rubs her neck.

~ ~ ~

Creeping at the other side of the lot, behind a rusty fence, is Rodney. He's turned out his flashlight, but he can see the figures well enough. When he pulled up near the plant he cut his engine a half-mile out and walked the rest of the way, still filled with adrenaline from watching Shane die. That fat fuck had it coming. Rodney has no intention of sharing the throne with anybody else.

He finds a small hole in the fence chains and crams himself in. A metal piece of the fence scrapes against his head and cuts him on his forehead. Blood trickles down into his eye. The three of them are a hundred or so feet away. The crazy redhead has his back to Rodney and is holding a gun to Norman's wife. Norman is facing Rodney's direction and he thinks he notices him. The redhead turns to see what Norman was looking at and Rodney runs behind an old car carrier. He stands with his back pressed hard against the cab. Norman had told him to come in and shoot the guy in the back of the head while he stalled him. Rodney keeps his body tight but turns to look. They're arguing. Jennifer is crying. Now would be a perfect time for him to go in and blow the maniac's brains all over her pretty hair and face, but Rodney stays still.

~ ~ ~

Norman reaches into his pocket and starts walking closer to Brett. "Stay where you are," says Brett, "or I will pull the trigger." But he doesn't. He loosens his grip on Jennifer's throat and points the gun towards Norman who's now running with his pair of brass knuckles shining on his hand. Jennifer runs off towards her car, but trips in a pothole and hits her face on the pavement. She gets to her hands and knees and crawls.

Brett gets off one shot, but Norman's already nearly on top of him and it goes high. With his left hand, Norman grabs the gun and points it away. Brett takes a hard right from Norman and his brass knuckles. He spits two molars and can't see straight. The hammer that was in his back pocket flies out. He hears it land to the ground as he falls over with Norman's weight pressing on his chest.

Straddling Brett, Norman holds the gun with one hand and smashes Brett's fingers with the other, cracking them with his brass. They're both grunting and cursing. Brett is grabbing at Norman's hair and trying to pull him off. He's still holding tight to the gun with what are now broken fingers. There's visible bone on his knuckles.

Brett lets go of Norman's hair and reaches out behind

him. At first all he can feel is the pavement, but then he gets one finger on the wooden handle of his hammer. With that one finger he pulls it just a little closer, sliding it a millimeter on the pavement while his other hand gets smashed to pieces. Then he gets another finger on it and then another. He holds it in his fist and closes his eyes. He turns it so the claw end is facing up and then he brings it up over his head and down into Norman's face in one fluid motion.

Norman screams. The claw has taken off his bottom lip and some of the flesh from his chin. Blood sprays onto Brett's face. He takes another swing with the hammer and this time he hits Norman in the thigh. The claw digs deep into flesh. Brett pulls it out and rams the top of the hammer underneath Norman's jaw and he falls back. Brett pushes Norman off of him and gets to his feet fast. With his broken hand he flings the gun. Dizziness overwhelms him so he doesn't quite know where he's throwing it, but it lands somewhere near Jennifer's car. He knows that Norman is screaming or at least making some sort of sound, but he can't hear anything aside from a ringing. He steps on Norman's hand, the one with the brass knuckles, and goes to work on his right knee, then his left. Norman's punching him the whole time with his free hand.

Once Brett let's up he stands over Norman in silence, staring down at him. He's splitting blood. Then he starts to laugh. "Jesus fucking Christ," he says, "I raped her. They held her down. It was over fifteen years ago. Is that all you wanted?"

Brett looks at the hammer in his hand. "Yeah." Then he smashes it down onto Norman's head and keeps doing it until there's nothing solid left.

~ ~ ~

Still behind the car carrier, Rodney watched the whole thing. It was sickening. The guy really is psycho, but still, he can't help but smile. It's all his now. He can run it all his way. No Norman telling him what to do. None of his white trash buddies to deal with.

The psycho's got to be dealt with though. It'll be easy; sneak up behind him and put one in his head. Then it'll be smooth sailing, mostly. But then he sees flashing police lights off in the distance. Everybody should be near the crime scene where the psycho killed Joe and Kenny. Who the fuck is this asshole?

Once he turns back his attention to where Norman's lying dead, the redheaded nut case has already stolen the cruiser and is speeding off to God knows where.

CHAPTER 29

For a half an hour, Sarah and Nate wait for Dan to leave the house. Police run in and out. A news crew has set up in the middle of the street. They've got a white van with a spotlight on the top of it, illuminating the scene, showing everyone the boarded up windows. There's a portly man with a camera on his shoulder and a bleached blonde woman in a pants suit. It's some local station nobody watches. Nate's got the windows rolled down. Sarah can only hear some of what blondie is saying. She keeps using the word rampage.

Dan comes out and walks to his car. It's on the opposite side of the news crew and the ambulances from where Sarah and Nate are positioned. "Go around the block and try to catch up," says Sarah. "Don't get too close, but don't lose him either." Nate punches the gas and the tires squeal. There's another car on the road slowing them down. Nate hops his sedan on the sidewalk to get around, tears tire tracks in somebody's manicured lawn. They get on to Route 27 and there's only one other car on the road, a cop car, about a quarter of a mile ahead. Sarah points. "There, follow him."

Lights and sirens are in one direction, but Dan's headed the other way. Nate scratches his head. "What the hell is he up to?"

~ ~ ~

Dan's impulse when he turns the key in the ignition is to follow the herd, but if there's one thing he's learned during his time on the Madison Park PD it's that impulse and herd following aren't always the best things to do. He'll have to follow along eventually, join in the chase, but he

169

wants to turn over every rock first. Plus, it'd be nice if he could do what Sarah asked and try to find Brett before everyone else does. There's no doubt they'll kill him and say they had no choice because he attacked first and nobody'll care enough to ask even one question.

Pulling off the street where everything went down with Joe and Kenny, Dan thinks quickly of all the places nearby somebody could go to hide. With so much blight, all the vacant lots, the warehouses and stores and factories that have sat empty for years, all the boarded up and foreclosed homes, there're endless options. Then he thinks real quick about his brother, a thought accompanied by an image of Shane when he was younger, before he'd squandered himself on drugs. The guy's always hanging around the old Ford plant, a place with enough rusted metal to hide behind for months. When he gets to the intersection with Route 27, instead of heading west like everyone else, he goes east.

The machinery of the plant looms high when he gets to it. There aren't any lights at the place, none still working anyway, but the place is lit up enough by the roads and the cars passing on them for Dan to see the old brick building topped with silver smoke stacks he hasn't seen puff anything since his oldest daughter was born. He drives around the place slowly, shining his spotlight on his passenger side on all the old vehicles. The light shines back at him off the metal and the windows.

Through the fence, he sees a car with its lights on. As he drives closer he can see Rodney standing there. Somebody's on the ground nearby.

"What the hell is going on?"

"That fucking psycho. Would you believe this shit?"

~ ~ ~

"A damn shame," says Nate when they approach the plant. "Shit like this all over the country." He's looking at a corrugated metal building towards the back of the property and making a *tsk* sound. "Now what the hell do all these people do for work now?" Sarah doesn't respond so he answers his own question. "Probably work at Wal-Mart. Fuck."

With squinted eyes, they both watch Dan pull his car through an opened gate in the fence. One of the buildings across the street is an old bar that, like the plant, shuttered long ago. Sarah remembers hearing stories in her youth about the place, about raucous fights with pool cues and broken bottles. She tells Nate to pull in there and shut the headlights off. He angles the car so they can see into the lot.

~ ~ ~

Dan's down on his haunches assessing the body. "Jesus. Was this Norman?" He knows the answer, but somehow feels obligated to ask.

Rodney's standing at the feet of the corpse. "His name tag was on the ground somewhere. Stepped on it when I came in. We'll get it when the sun's up a little more."

"You radio it in?"

There's no answer from Rodney. Dan's about to ask again when he feels the business end of Norman's firearm against the top of his skull. Before he can react the bullet's in his brain.

~ ~ ~

Nate pounds his fist on the steering wheel. "Aw, no, man. What the fuck is up with this place?" He puts his foot on the break and shifts the car into drive. "I'm getting us the hell out of here. There is nothing else we can do. Shit. Nothing."

Sarah opens the glove box. "You can do whatever you want, but you're letting me out." She ruffles her hands through the papers Nate has in the compartment and comes out with the gun. "And I'll get this back to you."

"Jesus. You *are* just as crazy as your brother. You even know how to use that thing?"

"You can wait and find out if you want. But I'm doing this on my own. Don't even think about getting out."

And Nate does wait. He watches Sarah run across the street like some sort of trained commando, the gun positioned in her hand against her thigh. She runs behind a car, crouches, sticks her head out for a second, and runs again. She stops again by the car carrier. Rodney must have heard something and he turns around. "No girl," says Nate, biting his knuckle. "You're gonna get yourself killed."

He gets out of the car while still watching Sarah, but before he can take a step she's out from behind the old rusty vehicle. She's got the gun pointed and held in two hands. Rodney's got his hands up in the air. The shot rings out and Nate sees a tiny spray of blood come out the back of his head. Rodney crumples to the ground. Sarah takes a step closer and fires another round in his face.

"Let's go," she says when she gets back in the car. She's wiping tears from her face. They're coming down freely. Nate's not sure how to react to the sobbing so he just keeps driving, keeps his eyes peeled for Brett. "He was a good guy, Danny, the guy that asshole killed. He didn't deserve that. He didn't do a fucking thing. Not a fucking thing."

"Let's find your brother and then get you both out of here. I'm gonna need to get rid of that gun too. Thank you very much about that."

"I'm sorry. I... just lost it I guess."

"You sure did. Fuck. I've never seen a woman do some shit like that."

"We're capable of more than you know."

"I guess so."

They see someone hobbling along on the side of the road, like they're injured. They're pants are torn. They get closer and realize it isn't Brett, that it's a woman. Nate picks up the gas. "No," says Sarah, "wait. I think I know who that is."

They pull up aside from the woman. Her face is bleeding. It looks like she tried to use asphalt for a slip-and-slide. Sarah rolls down her window. "Jennifer Kyle?"

At first she keeps walking, picks up the pace in fact. Then she realizes who it is that's talking and stops cold. She puts her hand in front of her face in a pointless effort to hide her wounds.

Sarah beckons her forward with her hand, tells her to get in. When she comes in the back seat and closes the door, she says, "I want... I want to get out of here."

Nate looks in the rearview mirror at her. "I think we can help you out with that."

CHAPTER 30

For the first time in his life Brett Bernauer has a plan. It's been gestating in his head on and off for his entire life. He's postponed it many times. He's told himself he was crazy for thinking it. When somebody famous does it people call them selfish. But the recent turn of events and his own recent actions have made it the only option he can see, selfish or not. Either this or spend the rest of his life in jail, watching as Sarah goes through more pain. What a waste of taxpayer dollars that would be. What a waste of oxygen. Then there's the possibility of a public trial.

It's a little surprising to Brett that the cops haven't blocked the local entrances to the Parkway, but they haven't. They will soon. Brett can hear the sirens. He gets on going south and rolls the windows down. It's early and past beach season so barely anyone else is on the road. It would be much better, he thinks, if he was making this last ride in his own truck, but that doesn't matter because it will be over soon enough.

When he was little they used to go over the bridge on summer days on their way to the beach. The kids would sit crammed in the backseat watching the waves out past the guardrails. They'd be talking about what they were going to do once they got there; swim, eat the sandwiches their mother made, play volleyball with other kids. Sarah would be sitting on one side of him going on about some girlie TV show Brett didn't care about or some friends at school he also didn't care about and Jonathan would be sitting on his other side listening to headphones, pretending he wasn't with them. Their parents would either be talking or listening to news on the radio. His father occasionally made crude comments while driving over the bridge about the amount of people that every year would get tired of living, pull their cars to the shoulder, and jump over the railing. Their mother would slap him in the thigh and tell him not to talk like that in front of the kids.

It's not like Brett is going over these memories because he thinks he's going to reunite with his dead family members. No, Brett harbors no expectations of what happens after life. His only hope is that he dies once he hits the water.

A few cars honk when he pulls over at the top. Nobody stops. Maybe it's too cold. Maybe he looks too crazy, bleeding everywhere. The wind is howling over the water. The ocean is beautiful. There are a number of seagulls out in the distance flying together, dropping into the water occasionally. The blue railing feels like ice when he puts his hands on it. He wonders how many other people have felt the railing like he's feeling it now, grabbing it tightly and lifting a leg over it. Then the thoughts stop and he looks at the water. It's a blue nothing he wants to be part of.

~ ~ ~

Sarah's looking at Jennifer. She's got her back turned and isn't watching where Nate's going. "I'm coming to some sort of bridge," he says. "I don't think he made it this far. I doubt it."

"Just get to the other side of the bridge and then turn around. We'll come back into town this way. It's too late to turn around now."

"Jersey roads. I swear."

Jennifer hasn't talked much. The only thing she said to Sarah was, "I'm sorry," but she didn't say for what.

Nate slams on the breaks. "Looks like the road is blocked ahead." He pauses and puts his hand over his mouth. There are police lights flashing ahead. When he turns to his right Sarah is already out of the car and running on the side of the road.

~ ~ ~

Out of the corner of his vision Brett sees a dozen or so police cars coming his way. Still holding on to the railing, he brings his other leg over. Then he lets go.

He falls with his eyes open. The wind is pulling at his skin, biting it. If he were to live afterwards he'd have burns just from that. The fall feels longer than it really is and he has time to think. Regret incubates in his brain and births inside of him like an unwanted child. Letting the air have its way with him, he's turned to face the sky and sees the bridge and everything else he let go of.

One last decision, this final one, and it's wrong too. Now that it's nearly over, the last thing he can do is force his body away from the world, against the wishes of the wind, and towards the fierce blue water.

When he hits the ocean he goes in feet first. The jolt is a thousand trucks into a thousand walls. The bones of his feet shatter like glass and his ankles snap. Both of his femurs break. His chest compresses and his lungs are punctured by jagged broken ribs and they start to fill with salt water. No one should survive that fall, but he has. Arms that are snapped like twigs flail in the water. There's nothing but inescapable pain, coursing through every inch of tissue and every nerve. Waves beat against his face as he tries to get his head above water. The instinct to live hasn't left him, as much as he wishes it had.

Looking through the current he can see the bridge and the cops that have congregated. If there's one consolation to going out like this it's that at least he won't die at their hands or in one of their cells. He made the choice. With that the pull of the water brings him down into the ocean.

~ ~ ~

Sarah doesn't see him jump. She's too late for that. What she does see though is Brett's head bobbing up and down in the waves. She sees him flapping his arms. There's no air in her lungs. The muscles of her legs turn to Jell-O and she falls to the ground with her hands sliding down on the blue metal railing her brother climbed up and jumped off of.

Nate comes up and crouches next to her. He puts his hand on her shoulder and lets her cry for a long time. When the wailing stops he tries to talk to her. "We have got to go now, alright." She swats his hand away and shakes her head no. "I know you don't want to, okay. I don't either. But we really need to go. You really need to go. Unless you forgot what you did." He looks around and then lowers his voice. "You killed a fucking cop. And whether he deserved it or not, you still killed a fucking cop, so you need to go, now."

~ ~ ~

Four hours later they're back in Pennsylvania, parked in front of a row home in Scranton. There are kids playing basketball in the street. Sarah's watching them and not saying anything. She was silent the whole ride other than sniffles. Jennifer's lying down in the backseat, waking up from a nap.

"This is it," says Nate, "You guys go inside, we sit down with Jeanine, and it's all done. You're in her hands from then on out. You won't see me again."

Jennifer sits up. "I'm ready."

Nate cocks his head. "You sure? This isn't something you can turn back from."

"I don't want to be associated with him or any of his shit."

"I get that." Then he turns to Sarah. "And how 'bout you?"

She's still watching the kids play basketball. One kid is trash talking the others. "No."

"No what?"

"No, I'm not going to do it. Bring me to a train station

and I'll figure the rest out from there."

He shakes his head and tries to look at Sarah's eyes but her head stays turned. "You are insane. Shit, are you for real? You know what they'll do to you if they find out what you did?" He angles his thumb back at Jennifer. "You are in far worse shit than she is just for being an accessory or whatever to whatever shit her husband was up to. And we don't even know that shit would stick for sure, but she still wants out. And you're telling me you don't"

Sarah turns around. Her eyes are red. "I don't want to run away. If it happens, it happens. I'm not running away."

CHAPTER 31

Nate has reopened his auto shop after a month off. Business has declined a little since then because people thought he was closed for good. His clients hadn't seen or heard from him.

But now the office of the auto shop is occupied by a friendly grey cat with half a tail. The kids love him. Nate's hoping that eventually that will help bring people back.

He hasn't talked to Sarah in weeks. The last he heard from her was in a text message. She left her job at the thrift store and was leaving Brooklyn. That was it. He told her to be safe and to drop him a line if she needed anything.

Jeanine has left a series of voicemails for him on his cell phone that he hasn't returned. They're all giving details about jobs and about people that have been abused. She says they need his help. On the last voice message she sounds pissed and wants to know what the hell his deal is.

Early on a Saturday morning, at a time he knows she won't answer the phone, he calls back and leaves a voice mail of his own. "I'm sorry Jeanine," he says, "but I can't do this anymore."

He's over at his shop and through the glass on the garage doors he watches the sun come up. The pink sky is so beautiful that he wishes someone else was with him so he wouldn't have to witness it alone.

A guy brought in an old Volkswagen late the other day. The thing was puffing out clouds of black smoke through the exhaust and bucking like an angry bronco on speed. Nate told the guy he'd do what he could. He came in on the weekend to get it over with. He wanted to turn it out quick, if he could. He figured the guy would have good things to say and maybe spread the word.

With the thing up on the lift and his hands up inside it, his mind wanders to Brett. It's a tragedy that the guy's life was one big fuck-up. Though he never said as much to him, Brett was the closest friend he'd ever had.

Halfway through the day, after he's replaced some hoses and the battery and fixed the water pump, he makes himself instant coffee and sits in his waiting room. The coffee is awful and he rests it on top of the magazines. When he calls Cynthia she's surprised to hear his voice, but doesn't seem angered. Hearing her voice makes him feel warm.

"I've been thinking, you know. A lot. You might not believe me, but I think I've changed."

She laughs, but it's a sincere and gentle laugh. There's no spite in it. "You're right. I don't believe you. If there's one thing I thought I had figured out about you while we were married it was the fact that you would never change. I didn't think that at first. It was one of those lessons learned the hard way."

Nate scratches his head and picks up the Styrofoam cup of coffee. "Yeah, I'll have to give that to you. For the most part I think you're right, but not now."

"Oh, you think so?"

"I do. I do. Some things happened, you know. They gave me perspective. I realize I've entered a new phase of my life. It's kind of like maturing."

Cynthia laughs again. "I always heard men took longer than women."

"Now c'mon, I'm serious now. I think I know when to let go of things a little. To let life take its own course, if you understand what I mean. Like, I can't determine everything."

Cynthia sighs. She's gone serious too now. "And why are you telling me this, Nate Bishop?"

"Because I'd like to show you that I've changed. I want you to see that I can be with you, but not be in control of you."

"You think so?"

"I do. Look, can we meet for coffee? Tomorrow? You want to see me again after that, great. You don't, that's cool too. Like I said, I can let things go."

"I can do coffee, Nate Bishop, but you listen, that's all I'm committing to. You text me the when and the where and I'll be there."

"I can do that. I can do that."

He unlocks the front door and walks outside to get some fresh air before he goes back under the Volkswagen. It's starting to get cold out, not the painful kind of cold that makes your bones hurt but the brisk kind that brings you energy and makes you feel alive. Nate stretches his hands up above his head and rotates at his hips. There aren't any clouds. It's the kind of day that feels like a new beginning. When he goes back inside he leaves the front door unlocked.

The clanking of all his tools is why he doesn't hear the door swing open an hour later. He doesn't hear the footsteps either. It doesn't occur to him that anyone else is in there with him until he feels the cold of a revolver against the top of his head.

"Get out from under there so I can see you when I kill you." Nate recognizes the voice. It's slurred a little like the guy's missing a few teeth and his jaw is cockeyed. When Nate rolls himself out from under the car he knows he's seen the face before too, but he can't place it. "Drop the wrench and stand up. Put your hands over your head." Nate does what he's told. His back is against his toolbox and remembers that his red pipe wrench is sitting on top of it.

"You sure you wanna point that thing at me?" says Nate. The man laughs in an uncertain kind of way, scratches his balding head. That's when Nate remembers who he is. It's the guy from their last job; from before he and Brett went to Madison Park. "Well, shit. If it isn't Stephen Balder. I have to say, I never thought I'd see your ass again."

Balder is nervous, shaking. "Oh, yeah, well here I am. Do you know that I had to eat everything through a damn straw for a month after what you and the other guy did to me?"

Nate smirks. "I didn't know, but I assumed as much." Then Nate brings down his right hand and pivots to grab his wrench. Before he has it in his hand Balder's gotten a shot off. Nate feels it pound through his upper back. The bullet goes into his shoulder blade, tearing the top part of his lung. As Nate turns, swinging the wrench, Balder pulls the trigger again and hits Nate in the chest.

With two bullets inside of him, Nate hits the gun out of Balder's hand and then goes to town on his head with the metal. The first hit breaks Balder's left cheek bone and pops out his eye. Blood is flooding into Nate's lungs and it feels as if the car on the lift has fallen on top of him. Balder crumples to the ground next to the tool box and Nate goes with him. He grabs him by the ears and slams his head against the sharp corner. He only has to do it twice before he knows that Balder is dead.

But Balder accomplished what he came for, dead or not. Nate is breathing his last breaths on the cold floor in a pool of blood. Something soft rubs against his face. For the last time, he opens an eye, red and watery, and he sees the cat that belonged to his dead friend. "Hey Al." With thumb and forefinger he messes the top of Al's head, runs a palm over his ear. Then he feels the cat's sandpapery tongue on his cheek as he closes his eyes.

CHAPTER 32

The *Star Ledger*, the only Jersey paper to carry anything that's not just rehashed text from a newswire, carried Nate's death with the headline "Friend of Madison Park Cop Killer Found Dead of Gun Shot Wounds." It was buried in the back under a story about how much the new Rutgers Football coach was making. Nate Bishop was found next to the body of an ex-high schoolteacher also suspected of murdering two men in Scranton that had connections to organized crime in Philadelphia. The ex-teacher died of blunt head trauma. The only family Nate had, it said, was an ex-wife in Easton.

Sarah read the story with white sheet rock dust on her hands, a respirator over her mouth and nose, and safety goggles pulled on top of her head. Fred brought the paper in to show her after he'd found the story while drinking his morning coffee in his truck. Sarah feels him standing awkwardly near her as she reads through, so she's conscious of her face and holds in her tears. No one is going to see her cry anymore, she's decided. "Did you know Nate?"

"I met him a few times," says Fred. "He was the only person your brother ever talked to. Drove him to jobs sometimes when that shit truck of his wasn't working." He's still chewing on a bagel he got at the 7-11. Jay is outside smoking a cigarette. "I knew they were up to something, you know, the way Brett would walk away whenever he got a phone call, like they were always planning. I should have said more than I did. Maybe things would have turned out differently."

Sarah flattens the paper in her hands and then rests it on the floor with the other pieces of old newspaper they're using as drop cloth as they paint the new walls they've put up. "They wouldn't have, so don't bother yourself with that."

Fred found Sarah on Facebook after he heard about Brett from the police. He reached out and told her that he'd help with whatever she needed, told her he wasn't upset about Brett stealing the guns. She took him up on the offer and asked if he'd help fix up her old house. No one would buy it after what happened. The only options were to tear it down or fix it up and move in.

"You gonna be alright, here?" asks Fred. "I mean after everything happened."

Sarah puts her hands on her hips and looks down. "We're gonna need some more white paint for the molding."

"Some more in the back of the truck. Gimme one sec and I'll go grab it. Just gotta use the restroom."

She ruffles the newspapers with her foot. "I got it." She's got a toolbox next to her and sticking out of it is Brett's hammer. "And I'll be fine. I mean, I've got no other option than to be fine. This is home. However bad it is, it's what I've known." Beatrice tried to talk her into to staying in Brooklyn and going back to school there, but Sarah told her she wanted to be in the old house. It was the only thing from her family she had left. That and the hammer.

Fred adjusts his jeans under his gut. "People around here aren't gonna give you crap?" She can tell he's got to piss from the way he's fidgeting, but he's holding it so he doesn't cut the conversation short.

Walking on her way to the front door, she says, "Oh, they will. Of course they will, but I could give a shit."

She says good morning to Jay as she walks outside to Fred's truck. There are kids walking to school. They look at her and whisper as they cross to the other side of the street. They're a boy and a girl. Maybe they're brother and sister, she thinks.

One more shot at life. That's all she's got in her. But she's going to squeeze it all out as best she can. She did take one piece of Beatrice's advice and signed back up for school at the local county college, nursing classes. Mostly because nursing's something somebody can do and cover all the bills on their own.

Against Beatrice's advice she's petitioned to adopt Dan's daughters. There's no telling which way the judge will decide, but she keeps in touch with the girls the best she can regardless, visits them at the foster family's place twice a week. It was awkward at first given they'd never met her, but things warmed up soon enough. The thought of the two girls growing up like that, with no real family, keeps her up at night. It's not like she's sure she'll be the best mother or anything like that, but she think it's only right that somebody that knew their father, at least a little, be the one that raises them.

When she turns around from the bed of the truck with the paint can she catches Jay staring at her ass. He acts like he was staring at some random section of pavement on the street. "Hey," he says, as he drops his cigarette and crushes it under his boot, "I'm sorry about your brother."

They're the first words she's heard from the kid. "Thanks. You know, he liked doing this sort of work. He would have enjoyed being here and doing this with us."

"Yeah, he was a good guy."

"No," she says, "No he wasn't, but I loved him anyway."

= = =

Thank you for reading.

Please review this book. Reviews help others find New Pulp Press and inspire us to keep providing these marvelous tales.

If you would like to be put on our email list to receive updates on new releases, contests, and promotions, please go to NewPulpPress.com and sign up.

ABOUT THE AUTHOR

Stanton McCaffery was born and raised in central New Jersey, where he resides with his wife and son. He has degrees in history and political science. His stories have been featured in Acidic Fiction, Heater Magazine, Out of the Gutter Online, and Between Worlds.

NewPulpPress.com

www.ingramcontent.com/pod-product-compliance
Lightning Source LLC
Chambersburg PA
CBHW070512260626
47161CB00004B/1526